wanted to win bad, but I felt like I should have stopped the game and asked those brothers if they knew what kind of game they were in. We were on the court living out our lives. I was playing my heart out, trying to get over—what were they doing? Had they been fooled? Did they think that the game was going to do for them whatever they wanted? That it didn't matter how they played as long as they performed the way they wanted?

An

"Yo, Drew, here's the story!" Jocelyn called me from the living room.

She and Mom were already sitting on the couch across from the television. Pops came out of the bathroom in his undershirt and started to say something, but Mom held her hand up.

"Wait a minute, honey," she said. "They're talking about that stickup on 126th Street."

Pops looked at me. There was a commercial on the television.

"It's coming up next," Jocelyn said.

A moment later a woman's face filled the screen.

What's happening with the youth of America? Well, if you're talking about the young people in our inner cities, the picture is far from pretty. Today two high school boys were involved in a vicious robbery and shoot-out in New York's Harlem community.

The image on the screen switched to a picture of the police stretching yellow tape across the sidewalk in front of a discount store.

At one thirty this afternoon, two boys, boys who should have been in school, attempted to hold up this store on 126th Street and Lenox Avenue. As they made their way from the store and down the busy street, they encountered an off-duty policeman, who immediately sensed what was going on. The two youths shot at the policeman, who returned fire. The result: a badly frightened and wounded clerk in the store, a sixteen-year-old in police custody, and a seventeen-year-old fatally wounded.

The country's educational mantra these days is "No Child Left Behind."

Tragically, this is yet another example of the growing number of children left behind on the cold streets of New York.

In Lebanon, negotiators have reached a tentative agreement . . .

Jocelyn switched channels.

"They didn't even give their names," Mom said.

"That's because they weren't eighteen yet," Pops said. "You can read about it in the papers tomorrow."

"It just tears me up to see young people wasting their lives like that," Mom said. "Every time you pick up the newspaper, every time you switch on the television, it's more of our young men either killed or going to jail. Lord have mercy! There just doesn't seem to be an end to it. Now there's a young man with all his life in front of him, and I know his parents wanted the best for him. Lying out on the sidewalk. It just . . . oh, Lord have mercy!"

Mom's voice was cracking, and I wondered why Jocelyn even had the story on. She knew how it upset Mom. She had always worried about me and Jocelyn, but then when my man Ruffy's brother was arrested right after Christmas, she got really messed around.

"I still think you children should finish school down south." Mom was on her feet. She had the towel in her hand she had been using to dry the dishes. "It's just safer down there."

Pops started in about how it wasn't any safer in Savannah, which is where my grandmother lived, than it was in Harlem. I went back to my room, and Jocelyn followed me in and plunked herself down on the end of my bed.

"Why don't you go to your own room, girl?"

"Why don't you let me borrow your cell until I get mine fixed?"

"No."

"Drew, you ain't got nobody to call. Let me use your phone."

"Those guys must have been on crack or something," I said. "Pulling a stickup in the middle of the day."

"So when do you pull your stickups?"

"Jocelyn, shut up and get off my bed."

"How long you think Mom is going to be upset?" she asked, not budging from the bed.

I took my sneakers off and threw them near her. "Yo, even when Mom's not acting worried, she's upset," I said. "I only got the rest of the year to go at Baldwin. You're the one she's going to send down south."

"I was thinking that maybe I should just go to Hollywood and start my career," Jocelyn said.

"I thought you were going to go to Harvard first."

"I could commute back and forth."

"And you could get off my bed so I can get some rest."

Jocelyn got up, picked up one of my sneakers, sniffed it, and then staggered out of the room.

The only time our neighborhood made the news was when something bad went down, and the talk in school was about the shooting and who knew the guy who had been killed. It was a hot subject in the morning but had cooled down by lunchtime. A helicopter had gone down in Afghanistan, and that made the front page of the newspaper. The main inside story was about some girl singer getting a divorce and accusing her husband of fooling around with her sister. That was good, because I knew Mom would be looking for news about the shooting. Everything that went down wrong in the neighborhood upset her. I could dig where she was coming from. There had been a time, a few years ago, when the shootings and all the drug stuff were just background noise. You heard about it happening, but unless some kid my age or Jocelyn's age was hit by a stray bullet, it didn't seem that real. But when I reached fifteen, it was boys my age being shot. Mom was always warning me to be careful and stay away from gangs. That's what she understood most—the gangs.

She knew I wasn't about gangs. I was about ball. Ball made me different than guys who ended up on the sidewalk framed by some yellow tape.

"Basketball is wonderful, Son," Mom would say. "And I'm sure glad you're playing sports instead of running the streets."

She would let it go at that, but I knew she had listened to people talking about how hard it was to make it in basketball. I knew that, too. But I also knew that even if I didn't make it all the way, I could cop some college behind my game. Everybody in the city who played any real ball knew my game was strong. James Baldwin Academy had almost made it to the regional finals in my junior year, and now, as a senior, I knew we had a good chance to make it. Last year I led the team in scoring, assists, and defense. The word was that there were a lot of scouts checking me out at the end of last year, and I knew they would be back this year. They always came after Christmas, when the deal got serious. There would be some guy recording your shoe size and how strong your wrists were and smiling when they asked you if you did any weed. They were smiling, but I knew what I had going on. All the real players told me to pick up my action during February, because that's when the scouts were sending in their reports. The thing was to make it to the tournaments in March, when the college coaches would be making their final reports.

My high school basketball career had been dope, but I knew I needed a strong finish, too. I remembered seeing documentaries on a couple of players headed for the big-time schools. Division I all the way. If I could deal big-time and get picked up by a smoking college program, I thought I could make it to the NBA. It was a dream, but it was a dream I could back up. Lots of dudes talked the talk and a few could even walk the walk, but I knew I was solid because I had big-money skills and my head was into the game. All I needed to do was to live up to my ability.

But every time something hard went down in the hood—some young brother got wasted, some kid got killed in a drive-by, or someone we knew got arrested—Mom got upset. I could dig it. She was about family all the way. When Tony got a fall, it shook Mom.

"Drew ain't Tony," Pops said. "He got more to him. Ain't you, Drew?"

"Yeah, Mom," I said. "I thought you knew that."

She smiled and patted me on the hand.

Tony is the brother of my best friend. If I needed a reminder, it was Tony. Everybody had thought he was all-world on the court, too. I knew in my heart that I was more than Tony. Maybe not on the court, but in real life. I had seen Tony hanging out on the corner and messing with the crack hos. It worried me some, because I wasn't digging anybody in the hood getting into a telephone booth and turning into Superman. But I believed in myself. When I looked around, I didn't see too many brothers believing in themselves. They were steady rapping sunshine, but you could see the weakness in their eyes when they had to stop rapping and walk away. It was like when you were on the court with a dude, and he was blowing smoke but backing off when the deal went down. I was fronting strong, but I knew that ball wasn't a done deal.

Ruffy Williams was Tony's younger brother. He was my main man and the team's center. He was usually happy, but when I met him in the hallway outside the media center, he looked pissed.

"What happened?" I asked.

"I bought an MP3 player from Ernie, and he told me he had downloaded over two hundred songs." Ruffy was six three, two inches shorter than me, but built like a tank. "So I hook up, and the only thing he's got downloaded is classical music."

Ernie Alvarez was a guard. He was usually cool but a little quirky. His father ran a television repair shop, and he was always getting used tape recorders and stuff that didn't work quite right. But he sold the stuff cheap, so it was okay.

"So we got practice today, right?"

"Yeah."

"How about we take some time out right after practice and kill Ernie?" I asked. "No big deal. We got other guys who can play guard."

"Hey, I heard we got two new players on the team," Ruffy said.

"Who told you that?"

"Needham. You know those two white guys we saw in the gym last week?"

"Yeah."

"Them."

I had seen the two guys around the school for a couple of weeks. One was small, maybe five ten, and played like he thought his game was hot. The other guy was big, my height, but broad. He played some ball during Phys. Ed. but I hadn't paid him a lot of attention. I did notice he had a slight accent.

I hate it when it's really cold outside and the windows are closed and it's stuffy in the school. Time dragged all day. I slid through the morning and made it into my afternoon English class with the clock pushing toward two. I was getting sleepy when Miss Tomita asked me to stand up and discuss the play we had been assigned to read. She didn't expect me to have my stuff together, so I sat at my desk looking all stupid while she got her steam up, and then I stood and started running it down.

"Okay, so *Othello*'s a play about this brother who was a general but was married to a white chick," I said. "The brother was uptight and worried that the chick was stepping out on him, and this guy he trusted, Iago, started whispering in his ear about what was going on behind his back. I think Iago didn't like black people."

"Mr. Lawson, Shakespeare described Othello as a Moor, but there's no reason to believe that his actual skin color was black. That probably would not have been acceptable in Elizabethan England." Miss Tomita was small, but when she was mad, she could make herself look bigger.

"The guy's picture on the cover showed he was a black man," I said.

"That is what the publisher assumed," Miss Tomita said. "We happen to be studying the author, not the publisher."

There were some kids goofing up as if I had done something really stupid instead of just making a simple mistake. I sat down and looked at the book cover again. I wondered why, if everybody else thought Othello was black, I wasn't allowed to think the same thing. I let it slide because you can't win with a teacher.

Everybody knew that Miss Tomita was the hardest teacher in the school. She was Japanese American and taught English and acted as if she loved every book that was ever written. As far as I was concerned, she had to be reading in her sleep to know as many books as she knew. I wanted to get my grades together, and English was my shakiest subject.

"What I'm going to do"—Coach Hauser, or House, as he liked to be called, ran his fingers through what was left of his hair as he stood facing the bleachers—

"is to carefully explain the philosophy of our team for the rest of this year. All those who disagree with the team's philosophy can save us some time by leaving as soon as possible, because they won't be playing with us. All those who agree with the team philosophy but can't manage to play it can leave, too. If there's not enough players left to make a team, then James Baldwin Academy will just skip the rest of the season."

He took his short, squat self over to the bench and picked up his travel bag. We watched as he took out some small bags and started tossing them out to us.

"Teams that make most of their baskets from within six feet of the hoop win most of the championships. That's a fact. And it's clear to me and to any student of the game. I am passing out tape measures to each of you so that you can understand what six feet means. Am I going too fast for anybody?"

"Yo, House, we've been kicking butt all season," Sky said, pulling on his crotch the way he always does. "Who you thinking we're going to be playing the rest of the season?"

"You're right. We did all right in the first half of

13

the season," House said. "But we still have half a season to go, and this time we want to get into the state finals."

"In other words, you need me to carry the team again," Sky said, smiling.

"What I need is for us to play both halves of the season," House said. "Team ball is going to get us where we want to go. I expect our big men, the two forwards and center, to score most of the points every game. What's more, I expect them to score within six feet of the rim. That's what we're going to be working for, and that's how the team will be playing. For our big men to be doing the scoring, they're going to have to do most of the shooting. Which means that our guards are going to have to set them up, and to pick up on the number of assists. These are simple ideas, but they will win ball games. Anytime we have a game, win or lose, in which the guards score the most points, I'm going to find out what went wrong and correct it. And if I have to sit people down to keep the team philosophy in mind, I will do that. Any questions?"

Nobody had any questions, but I wondered what was bugging House. We had a dynamite squad last year and had played good team ball. I figured he was just letting us know he was serious about moving on, and I was cool with that.

In the bags that House gave us were the tape measures he'd mentioned. All of them were exactly six feet long. Okay, I got the point. Last year it was two passes before every shot. This time it's work the ball inside more. No big deal.

The Baldwin Chargers would start the year with twelve to fourteen players. Usually by midseason we had lost three or four of the original guys because they had messed up in school or moved out of the neighborhood. When I was a freshman, they even had a kid who dropped out because he got stabbed halfway through the season. We also added players, so when I saw two new guys in uniform, it didn't mean much. Neither did the coach's talk. I loved ball and knew I was going to bust it, whatever joint he was running.

House told us to get into layup lines, and I felt myself getting excited. I liked everything about playing ball: the way the ball sounded hitting the floor when the gym was empty, the shine of the lights off the polished boards, the smell of the locker room, everything. What I liked most was the feel of the ball in my hand, the pebble grain against my fingertips.

"Hey, Drew, we got two new white players." Ricky Montez was behind me in the layup line. "I guess they didn't have to try out for the team."

"Maybe they're in an affirmative action program," I said.

When it was my turn to cut for the layup, I moved down the side of the lane, pivoted off my right foot, got the pass, and put the pill up softly with my right hand. I knew the first one who dunked was going to catch it from House. It was Sky.

Sky is a stone clown. He would be a better ballplayer if he didn't do two things—fool around so much and hang out drinking beer all the time. He got the ball about nine feet from the basket, did his little foot shift like he always did when he was going for the dunk, and then went up.

Bam! Sky had that big grin on his face and House was turning red blowing his whistle. What cracked everybody up was that Sky started running around the gym doing laps even before House could tell him how many he had to do.

We did layups for a long ten minutes; then we did box-out drills for twenty minutes with House and Joe Fletcher, the assistant coach, throwing balls against the backboard. One of the white guys was soft looking. I felt the other dude, the one House kept putting on me, was checking me out for some reason.

"Watch your elbows, Drew!" House called out. "You're not strong enough to hold him out without fouling?"

I went to the bench and sat down. House came over and asked me what was wrong.

"I got a cramp in my side," I said, not looking at him.

"In your side or in your style?" he asked. Then he walked away.

I didn't like that remark, but that was the way House did his business.

After the box-out drill we had loose-ball drill before calling it a day. Ruffy caught up with me at the door and asked what was going on with House.

"I don't know," I said. "We were good last year. Maybe he thinks we can go all the way this year."

In the locker room everybody was kidding around, cracking jokes, like they always did. All the guys on the team like playing ball, and that made being on the team a tight roll. Nobody was sweating House's new philosophy, because we had all heard a thousand of his theories before.

Fletcher got us all quieted down and told everybody to give his name and position so the new men would know who we were.

"Needham Brown, forward."

"Sky Jones, star center."

"Ernie Alvarez, guard."

"Drew Lawson, guard."

"Ruffy 'the Man' Williams, center."

"Colin O'Brien," the small white guy said, "guard."

"Malcolm Small, forward."

"Tomas Dvorski, forward," the other white player said. He pronounced his name as if he was saying *toe*-mus.

"Abdul Ghoia, forward."

"Bobby Rice, lover!"

We all shook hands and said "Hey" to the new players. There weren't that many white guys in

Baldwin, but we didn't have any problems, so it was all good. I showered, got dressed, then went over to where Fletch was counting supplies.

"What you think?" I asked. "We going to do it the second half of the season?"

"Depends on how deep your game is," he said.

"It's deep, my brother."

"We're going to find out just how deep," Fletch said, looking up at me. "Hope you can tell me that at the end of the year."

Fletch is one of those quiet guys who know the game and leave all the rah-rah stuff home. They said he could rock it back in the day, but he didn't run his mouth about it.

I knew my game was deep enough. Ball is me and I'm ball. It doesn't make any difference to me what people talk about when they say that all brothers want to do is hoop and rap.

I found Ruffy and asked him what he thought about the team, and he said he was surprised that House didn't have us scrimmage with the white boys.

"I need to find out if I got any competition," he said.

We walked down the street together with me thinking that if House was serious and Fletch was serious, maybe they thought it was going to be a big year for us.

The way I figured, the Chargers were just a little short on D and about four points shy of Big Time, which is cool for a public school that doesn't recruit like some of the prep schools in the area.

When I got home, my father was talking about how he needed to join a gym and get into shape again.

"It's about time you tried losing some of that belly," I said.

"That's what I've been trying to tell your mother," he said. "She's talking about me walking to work. Now, how would I look walking all the way from here down to 128th Street and Amsterdam Avenue?"

"Richard, you know if you join a gym, you're going to go for two weeks and then all the money you invested in it is going to be lost," Mom said.

"How are you going to feel if I die of a heart attack because I'm out of shape?" Pops came back.

"You can die of a heart attack looking like

Superman," Mom said. "Then all the people will just be saying how good you look in your casket."

Twenty-two blocks, which was how far our house was from the bus garage, wasn't that far a walk, but I knew my father wasn't going for it. He needed to do something, though, and he knew it.

The principal of Baldwin Academy is Dr. Cornelius Barker. Everybody calls him Dr. Doom because once a year he shows up in a white suit, white socks and shoes, white shirt, and white hat, and you know that is the day when he is going to call anybody who's really been messing up into his office and give them the bad news. Right after Christmas it had been my turn.

I got into the outer office and had to sit on the bench with Stringy-Hair Patty Thompson, Don't-Give-a-Crap Charles Stover, Don't-Take-a-Shower John Poole, and Sean Conway, who was too busy selling bootleg videos seven days a week to even come to school half the time. When it was my time to go into the office, Dr. Barker gave me five and asked me how I was doing.

"I'm all good," I said. "I'm not failing anything."

"Hey, I know that." Dr. Barker leaned back in his chair. "You know I keep my eye on you. I know my buddy Steve Joyner down at Johnson C. Smith called you about signing a National Letter of Intent. He said you weren't too interested."

"Yo, Dr. Barker, if I sign, it means I *got* to go to Johnson C. Smith or I can't play anywhere else for a year," I said.

"It also means an athletic scholarship," Dr. Barker said. "Where else did you apply to?"

"University of Washington," I said. "That's my dream. Then Kean University over in New Jersey, 'cause their coach—he used to be at St. Peter's—likes my game. Arizona, because I like their game. And Virginia Union is my fallback because a friend of mine said that a lot of people check out their actions. Plus I'm going to hook up a few last-minute applications when my folks get the money."

"Okay, two of your picks are checking you out because of me," Dr. Barker said. "That's J. C. Smith, where I went to school, and Kurzinsky at Kean, because I knew him from Jersey City. Let me tell you this, young brother: The world keeps spinning whether you're ready to make a choice or not. Be careful what you're walking away from."

"I know where you're coming from, and I'm heavy on it, sir."

"I hope so," Dr. Barker said, standing up.

Dr. Barker was for real, and his looking out was serious. I knew he was talking about maybe hooking me up with some black college. He had done it before, but I also knew that all the heavy ballplayers, black or white, were going to the big schools. I didn't just want to go to college, I wanted to play ball in college. Okay, maybe I wanted to go sit on some campus and read about myself in the paper. What my dream really was—and I didn't want to lay it out in front of Dr. Barker—was to play in the NBA and then maybe do a commercial for a smoking car. I'd probably have to learn to drive, but I knew I could hook that up.

What the guys knew was that my game was money. All I needed was to show proper and we would come in either first or second in our division. We were already six and one with just a fall to Bryant. Bryant was seven and zip with half the season over. We were going to play them one more time, and if we could beat them, we had a shot to be numero uno. The trouble was that Bryant had a monster squad, and in the first game they caught us napping and beat us even without Boogie, their best player.

James "Boogie" Simpson had game and then more game behind that. The sucker was unreal. He was six four, midnight black, laid-back, and always smiling like he knew something you didn't. And what he knew was what he was going to do to your game if you brought it onto his court. Bryant had beaten us when Boogie was out with some kind of infection. When he got better, he just resumed busting every team he faced.

The word was that Duke and Marquette had been asking about Boogie. When they faced us, the dudes with the pads and measuring tapes would be watching him, and that was going to be my chance to show what I could do. If Duke tapped me on the shoulder, even Dr. Barker would sit up and take notice.

There were three reporters and a photographer at practice the next afternoon.

"They're interviewing that white dude," Sky said.

"What for?"

"I guess because he's that white dude," Sky came back.

They were talking to the new guy, Tomas. When Sky said they were interviewing him because he was white, the other white guy, Colin, gave him a look, but he didn't say anything.

We shot around a little, and Fletcher had us doing layups while we were jumping over a heavy punching bag, which nobody liked.

"Yo, coach, suppose we fall on the bag and ruin our whole career?" Abdul asked.

"If you can't even avoid a punching bag, you're not going to have an NBA career," Fletch said.

"They don't do this in the NBA," Ruffy said.

"Yeah, they do," Fletch said, "only they use those expensive bags. They call them assistant coaches."

House and the new white player finally finished the interview and called us together. We ran wind sprints for ten minutes while some guys took photos, then we did calisthenics with dumbbells for ten minutes, then more wind sprints. All the players were into the sprints, but Ruffy and Abdul were doing some serious heavy breathing.

The drills running backward were usually fun, but House had his serious face on and was yelling at everybody, so we played along. Then we did some sidestepping and some more wind sprints. After the newspaper guys left, Ricky asked the coach why they had shown up for a practice. He got put off big-time.

I dug the newspaper guys being around. What I knew was that if I didn't get any press and the college coaches didn't know about my game, I wouldn't be getting any phone calls. The real deal was that you either got onto a Division I team, the big schools, or the National Basketball Association didn't want to talk to you.

"Hey, man, which is my good side?" Needham Brown came real close and put his face near mine. "I don't want no lame pictures over my stats in the paper."

"Square business, man," I said. "You don't have a good side."

Needham looked at me as if I were crazy. The thing was, the dude thought he was good-looking, which was like a bad joke. Needham looked like one of those little jumpy dogs with big eyes that can't get their bark straight. The thing was the guy could pull some serious chicks, though. I couldn't figure it.

We did another drill, jumping with one-pound weights in our hands, and then House sent us into the locker room.

"It goes like this," he said. "You saw those reporters out there. This year the papers are going to be doing more stories on high school ball. Those newspaper reporters are going to keep coming around as long as we're winning. We start losing and nobody is going to pay us any attention. And we're going to keep winning as long as we understand what we're doing on the court and play the kind of ball we're supposed to be playing."

What I was wondering was if the reporters were interested in the team, as House said, why were they only talking to the white player? What was that supposed to mean?

On the way out Tomas came over to me and asked me why the team was called the Chargers.

"They call us the Chargers because we buy our own uniforms," I said, feeling stupid even as I said it. "We don't pay cash, we just charge the uniforms and then take them back at the end of the season."

Tomas didn't go for it, I could tell. Meanwhile, Needham cracked up the way he did every year when we told that to a new man. It wasn't even funny, but we did it every year anyway.

I wondered why Tomas had come over to me. I thought that House must have told him something about me or *somebody* told him something about me. I was the main man on the Chargers. Maybe he thought he was going to take the team over.

With high school ball you usually have one dude who can bust it and three or four dudes who can play some. If you get two dynamite dudes, then you can smell a league championship, maybe even move a little higher. You can't do much in the all-state finals on the East Coast, because all the prep schools go out and recruit the best ballplayers. Baldwin was all right, though. Baldwin was always in the hunt for the division championship.

After practice Ruffy grabbed the downtown bus, and I caught up with Tomas and Needham. Needham was running his mouth about how some new woman he had met loved him and even gave him money.

"She's about twenty-two," he said. "I think she

works part-time as a model and part-time in the post office."

Yeah.

"Yo, Tomas, where you from, man?" I asked.

"Prague," he said, reaching out his hand. "You know the Czech Republic?"

"Not really."

"It's in eastern Europe," Tomas went on. "I've been in the United States for two and a half years."

"You play ball in—where did you say you were from?"

"Prague."

"Yeah, you play ball there?"

"Sure," he said. "I also play ball here in the gym in Queens last year. You know Flushing?"

"Yeah, I do," I said. "Where you live now?"

"On 142nd Street, near Broadway," he answered.

I said good-bye to Tomas on the corner, and Needham ducked into the corner store. He said he had to pick up some toothpaste for his grandmother, but I knew the dude was probably getting some chips and didn't want to share them. No problem.

Then I started thinking about Tomas again. Why had the reporters interviewed him and not all of us?

The only thing I could think of was that House had told them that Tomas was the man to watch on the Chargers. There was definitely some stink in the air.

House had probably seen Tomas play in Flushing. The coach lived near Shea Stadium and sometimes refereed games at the community center. Most of the good players who came from out there were either Chinese or Korean. They were quick, but they didn't have much size. Tomas might have looked real good against smaller players.

Got home from school and Jocelyn was pissed. The girl stays mad.

"What's your problem?" I asked.

"I'm supposed to ask two of my friends and two people in my family why George Washington was selected as the first president of the United States." Jocelyn sucked her teeth after every other word.

"Yeah, so what's wrong with that?"

"I think we're all supposed to say something stupid and then my teacher can tell us his answer and go back and tell all his friends how slow black people are," she said.

"So why was he the first president?"

"Because they had put his picture on a one-dollar bill and he asked how come he was on the one and Benjamin Franklin was on the hundred-dollar bill," she said. "They had to think fast, so they said because he was going to be our number-one president."

"Jocelyn, that is so retarded!"

"You want me to fix you something to eat?"

"Yeah," I said. I was a little surprised Jocelyn was going to make me something, but I figured she was upset, so I sat down at the table.

"Peppers and eggs?"

"Okay."

There were some green peppers in the fridge, and Jocelyn got them out and started cutting them up. She was good in the kitchen because she had fast hands.

"If he's supposed to be teaching me something, then go on and teach it," she said as the knife chopped away. "Don't be taking time out to diss me on the side and then acting like I don't even know you're dissing me."

"What did you get in history last year?" I asked.

"And wait a minute; I thought your history teacher was a brother."

"He's not a brother," Jocelyn said. "He's an African Somerian."

"What's that?"

"Some of the time he's acknowledging his African heritage and some of the time he's holding his breath and pretending he's white." Jocelyn put the peppers on the fire and sprinkled in some minced garlic and it was smelling good. "People like that end up saying how slavery wasn't so bad."

"You're too hard on the dude," I said.

Jocelyn put on the television and switched on the black station while the peppers and garlic cooked. There was a rap video on, made by some chick who just got out of jail.

"You think she's hot?" she asked.

"Hey, where's the Czech Republic?" I asked.

"It's right under Poland," she said. "You know where Poland is?"

"No."

"You find Germany on the map, then you go a little to the right—that's east; then you run into the Czech Republic," Jocelyn said. "It's a little smaller than New York State, so you know it's not big-time or anything."

"I guess."

"Why did you ask?"

"This new guy on the basketball team is from there," I said.

She scrambled the eggs in a dish, then poured them over the peppers and garlic. I watched her stirring, giving the eggs a half flip, and then letting it sit while she got a plate from the closet. By this time Pops had caught the smell and came into the kitchen.

Jocelyn put the plate of peppers and eggs in front of me and handed me a knife and fork.

"They look okay?"

"They're better than okay," I said.

"Take a mouthful right now," she said.

I took a mouthful.

"So you going to loan me thirty-five dollars for a new memory chip?"

Jocelyn is just stone wrong and she knows it.

The first game in the second half of the season was a non-league game against Wadleigh. Wadleigh was a trip because the whole team was made up of skinny Latino brothers who could out-and-out fly. If they got you in their running game, you were over before you started, because they never got tired. The only way to stop them was to get an early lead and then control the boards so they couldn't run. It also helped to beat on them a little if the refs let you get away with it.

We went downtown to their raggedy-butt gym, checked out their fly girls, and had just started our warm-ups when Ricky came over and told us who was starting. House had put both the white boys in the starting lineup with me, Ruffy, and Sky. Ricky was mad big-time, and so was I. On the bench before the game House came up with some noise about getting in as many combinations of players as possible because it was a non-league game.

"I want to see what works and what doesn't," he said.

"You didn't see what worked in the first games?" Sky asked.

"I'm still trying out things," House came back. "Don't worry about it."

I knew the guy who was supposed to be guarding me. He lived in the Bronx and ran with the Latin Deuces. He had a funny way of holding his face, and his cousin, a foxy mama I tried to get next to once, told me he had been shot in his face when he was nine. I called him Stoneface behind his back, but I didn't mess with him too tough because the dude acted like he might have been a little off.

Wadleigh got the ball first, and House called for a one-two-two zone, which is seriously wack against a running club. While you're falling back into a zone position, they're going past you to the hoop. Stoneface brought the ball down, faked toward Colin, then flew past him and made a layup over Sky. They had the first deuce.

On defense a little dark-haired guard took the ball away from Colin before he got to half-court. They had four points.

Just about the whole first quarter was Wadleigh's show. They were doing anything they wanted to and we were flatfooted. Colin couldn't play any D at all and was doing his toreador moves, watching guys go past him.

Meanwhile, I'm checking out Tomas. What I saw was that he knew how to use his body, blocking out on offense and being kind of strong on defense. But he never got off the floor. It's okay to block out, but you have to jump or guys will go over you, especially if they're quick enough to roll to your side. On offense he had a few moves and was strong to the basket, but he wasn't getting up. Twice his man knocked his shot away, and once, when Tomas made a weak fake and tried an easy shot from under the hoop, the defensive guy jumped up and grabbed the ball in midair. When he did that, all the girls from Wadleigh started cracking up on the sideline.

House kept calling the same two plays over and over. Me and Colin were bringing the ball upcourt slow, passing in to Ruffy or Sky at the high post, then slanting across looking for the soft pick high while Tomas set up deep and rolled away from the ball looking for the inside pass.

When we weren't doing that, we were bringing Ruffy way out to set a high pick, crossing the off guard out near the foul line, and trying to set up a backdoor or a chippy for one of the forwards. Either way I could see that House was setting up the game so that Tomas would look good.

The guys on Wadleigh saw what was going down and were eating it up. I asked House to switch to one-on-one so I could guard Stoneface, but he wouldn't. As we got to the end of the first quarter, it was Wadleigh 26 and us 14. Our guys were down and Wadleigh was having fun.

The second quarter went the same way. It was Wadleigh doing what they wanted to do and us playing like we were at practice or something. I tried setting a few picks for Colin, but he ignored them and went for the inside play the way House told him.

Near the end of the half Wadleigh hit a couple of threes and were nonchalanting the whole deal. I hate it when guys start acting like the game is over and they're too good to lose. Then Stoneface got into a switch with their center, faked inside, and when Ruffy followed him out of the paint, threw up a pretty hook and made it. The guys from Wadleigh goofed big-time on that. They weren't showing us any respect. I knew what House was doing. He was working out his game plan and, because it wasn't a league game, didn't care if we lost or not. I'd take the loss, but I wasn't giving up the respect.

Colin passed me the pill on the inbound and stopped to wait for it back, but I started downcourt. Stoneface picked Colin up at half-court and came down with him. I stopped ten feet behind the key, pointed at Stoneface, and beckoned for him to come on out and get me. He wasn't going to let that slide and came over. My man switched to Colin.

Stoneface is quick and he's real strong. He's got this way of holding his hands up about shoulder high to make you think he's not going for the ball, but he's moving his body into you and putting you off-balance so you can't get around him. I saw that but I knew I could beat it.

"Yo!" I threw a head fake to the right, the first one that Stoneface had seen all day, and came back hard to my left, dipping under his shoulder.

I knew I had half a step, maybe less, and Stoneface was going to be coming. I went hard down the left side, planted on the line, and went up and across the lane and threw it down from the far side.

It was sweet and everybody in the gym knew it. Ruffy screamed, and Abdul, who had come in for Sky, fell down like he had fainted.

The ref blew the whistle and said something to Abdul about taunting, but he didn't call a technical. House called a time-out. When we got to the bench, he was looking up at the clock. There was still more than a minute to go in the half.

"Drew, sit down!" he barked.

I knew House was pissed, but I just shrugged it off. As far as I was concerned, I hadn't done anything wrong.

I didn't play at all in the second half. The guys in the game kept looking over toward where I sat. They were feeling for me, and I knew they were confused. I had busted Stoneface and it had lifted the whole team, and then I was being punished for it. That sucked big-time.

The final score was 66–52.

"We will play this game the way I say we will play it," House said in the locker room, "or we won't play it at all."

The whole team was tense as we dressed. All the old guys came over to where I was sitting and told me how foul the crap was about sitting me down. The team bus was parked just off 14th Street, and we put the gear on it. When I saw House sitting in the back, I made it a point to sit up front. Fletch came over and told me that House wanted to see me.

"I don't want to see him," I said.

"You mad about sitting?" Fletch asked.

"Yeah, I'm mad," I said. "You think that was right?"

"I think he's the coach and has the job of running the team," Fletcher said, sitting next to me. "Long as he's the coach and you're not, he tells you how to play."

"And all the Uncle Toms on the team are supposed

to go along with him," I said. "That's the way it's supposed to go? Or that's just the way you glad to see it go?"

He turned and just looked at me. I knew I shouldn't have said that bit about Uncle Toms, but I was still mad.

"I know how deep I am, boy." Fletcher's voice was low, his words slow. "Do you know how deep you are?"

I didn't really know what he meant by that, but I turned away and looked out the window as the bus pulled off.

What I knew in my heart, as the bus made its way toward the West Side Highway, was that House was messing with me, with who I really was. When I was on the court, I was a different person than I was sitting in class or just walking down the street. House knew that as well as anybody. When I walked down the street I was ordinary, maybe even ordinary in a not-much kind of way. Sometimes when I hit the neighborhood and saw dudes a little older than me nodding out on the corner or standing around waiting for something to do with their lives, it made me feel terrible because something deep inside told me I was headed in the same direction they were. All those bad feelings, the not being much, the struggle with school, all of it left me when I was on the court.

The bus stopped at the school, and we took out the equipment bags and Abdul and Needham carried them inside. I started down the hill.

"Hey, Drew!"

I turned around and saw Tomas coming toward me.

The big white boy ambled over to me, walking with one shoulder a little higher than the other. I hadn't noticed that before.

"Hey, Tommy," I said.

"*Toe*-mus!" he said.

"Whatever."

"No, Tomas."

"Tomas."

"So you're mad that you didn't play," he said, pointing to his eyes. "I saw that."

"Yeah, well, I was," I said.

"Why don't you come to my house," he said. "I have a shirt from my team in Prague I'll give you. Okay?"

"What?"

"You don't have a shirt from Prague," he said. "Come with me and I'll give it to you."

"No, that's okay, man."

"We're friends, right?" he asked, sticking out his hand.

"Yeah."

"So I don't live too far," he said.

I didn't feel like going home with Tomas, but I didn't feel like just walking away, either. If anybody or anything gets in my face, I don't back off. That's not me.

"Yeah, okay," I said.

When you look down into the valley along 145th Street, all you see is black faces because that's all that lives down there. Up the hill, especially past St. Nicholas, you're liable to run into anything, especially lately with all the white people buying houses in Harlem. I wondered if Tomas was rich. He didn't look rich, but you couldn't tell with some people.

All the time we were walking, Tomas was talking about Stoneface. He was saying that he wasn't that good and that Wadleigh wasn't that hot a team.

"They were good enough to beat us," I said.

"Well, that's pretty good," he said.

As we walked, I was wondering if House had told him to come over and talk with me. My mind was working overtime and I was sniffing the air for clues to what was going on. I didn't trust Tomas, but I wasn't going to back off, either.

Tomas spoke well. Just once in a while he would pronounce words differently than I expected. I asked him about it and he said he had studied English in Prague and that his family had lots of friends who spoke English.

We walked down to 142nd Street off Broadway. Tomas lived in a brownstone, and I figured his family must own it until I saw there were three bells over the mailboxes. We walked upstairs to the second floor. He knocked on the door and called his name out.

The peephole clicked. A woman opened the door and looked at Tomas, then at me, and then back to him.

"This is my friend Drew," he said.

I followed Tomas into the apartment. It was okay, but nothing special. There were lots of books lying around and odd-looking pieces of colored glass. The woman asked us if we wanted something to eat and I said no, but we were already headed for the kitchen.

"Please sit down," the woman said to me.

"My mother, Anna," Tomas said.

"He didn't think I was your girlfriend," she said with a little crooked smile.

Tomas's mother was all-right-looking, no make-up, real plain clothes, as if she didn't care about her appearance. She had dark blond hair, blue-gray eyes, a thin mouth, and a large forehead that made her look a little like an old-fashioned doll. She sat at the table and folded her hands in front of her.

"Would you like some tea?" she asked after I had sat down.

"Sure," I said, being sociable.

"Go buy some tea," she said to Tomas.

"Hey, I don't need the tea," I said.

She made him go out to buy it and told me to sit down when I was going to go with him. The way she told me to sit sounded like she thought she was my mother.

"So you are a basketball player, too?" she said when Tomas had taken some money off the refrigerator and left.

"Yes."

"My husband used to play basketball in Prague," she said. "Mostly he played football—you call it soccer over here—but he also played the basketball. Do you know anything about the Czech Republic?"

"Not really," I said, trying to remember where Jocelyn had said it was.

"It's in eastern Europe," she said. "It used to be part of Czechoslovakia, but we broke the country in two and now it's the Czech Republic. I don't know if that's good or not, but that's what it is."

"Your husband still play ball?"

"No, he played when he was young," she said. She nodded as if she was agreeing with herself. "But in 1977, during the struggle with the government, he was wounded and put in jail. His legs were hurt and he walked with a cane until he died."

"I'm sorry to hear about that," I said. "What did he do?"

"He was a teacher," she said.

"No, I mean what did he do to go to jail?"

"David wrote a column in the university news-paper," she said. "He wrote how we wanted to have more freedom and more choices in our schools. It was only a small paper, but everybody on that staff went to jail. Including me."

"You were in jail?"

"Don't smile," she said, suddenly serious. "I was in jail for two weeks. When they took the men on the staff to jail, the women protested, too. We blocked traffic; some of us threw rocks at the state police. We had the scent of freedom and wanted it badly. It wasn't bad, because they didn't hit the women. They knew if they beat us up, it would just make more people mad at them."

"You didn't think they would put you in jail?"

"We knew, but we also knew we had to do something," she said. "You can't let them take away your freedom. You don't have anything else. When they finally let my husband out of jail, he was pretty bad off."

"I never heard of anybody going to jail for writing in a newspaper," I said.

"Americans don't know about things like that," she said. "You're a very busy people."

Tomas came back with the tea and his mother made it. She said she had been an artist in Prague, sculpting with glass.

"One day I'll get back to it," she said, pouring the tea.

"I can see why you like the United States better than Prague," I said.

"There's nothing wrong with this country and I like it very much," she said. "But I don't like it better than my own country. We lost everything in the floods a few years ago. Half of Prague was under water, just like in your country where the black people live."

"New Orleans," I said.

"We lost our house, our books, our computer, our clothes." She turned toward Tomas.

"We have a cousin here," he said. "He found my mother a job in a hotel. That's why she works at night."

The tea was terrible. They didn't put any sugar in it, and I didn't know if they had any so I didn't ask.

I liked Tomas's mother, but I wasn't comfortable around her. She had done things that I had never known anybody doing before, like going to jail for throwing rocks at the police, or writing for a school paper, or making stuff out of glass. I didn't know any white people who had been in jail, period.

Tomas got the shirt and gave it to me. I hung out

for a while, mostly listening to his mother talking about life in her country. I realized they didn't have much, probably not as much as my family.

Tomas let his mother do most of the talking. Sometimes it was almost as if he were listening to her stories for the first time, too. I knew he must have known most of it, but I guess it was funny to hear your mother talking about throwing rocks at cops no matter where you came from.

What I got from the whole scene was that Tomas was scoping the tension on the team the same as I was. He was trying to cool it down, and I thought that was good, but it still didn't explain what was going on.

I got home and showed Mom the shirt I got from Tomas and told her about having tea with them and about his mom.

"Do they look dangerous or anything?" Mom asked. "His mother sounds like a radical."

"No, she ain't radical," I said.

Jocelyn took the shirt and said she was going to find out what USK PRAHA, which was written across the front, meant.

I lay down across my bed, felt around for the

remote, and started flipping through channels. I wondered if House was trying to make Tomas the star of the team just because he was white. The Chargers weren't broke—why was he trying to fix us with some guy who was going to mess up the whole team?

There was current events homework to do, and I thought about it as I lay down. I had downloaded some new jams and thought I would check them out while I went over the homework.

My mind drifted to English. I thought of Miss Tomita saying that Othello was probably not black the way we think about black people today. The way I figured it, Shakespeare wouldn't have put him in the play if being black wasn't an issue. And why was Iago messing with him if it didn't have anything to do with race?

I hadn't read the whole play yet, but I did remember Othello telling the chick about his life. Maybe that's what made Iago mad. He didn't have anything to run down about who he was and resented my man Othello.

I decided that no matter what Miss Tomita said, I was going to think of Othello as a stone brother.

House said he was going to add something new to each practice. The big thing in the next practice was a ballhandling drill where he had us going up and down the court around cones dribbling two balls at the same time. I didn't think much of that at first until I saw how some of the guys couldn't handle the ball as easily as I thought they should. I checked out Tomas, and he did all right for a big man.

I kept away from House. He was making notes on his clipboard, something he hadn't done before. He was letting us know he was serious, but I still didn't know what he was trying to do.

We ran some wind sprints and then a wing drill.

"The guys on defense, bring your fists up under your arms and hold out your elbows as if you had wings," Coach called. "Anybody who passes you and they're outside your elbows does five laps around the gym."

The object of the wing drill was to go at a defender as hard as you could but as close to his body as possible. If you went by him close, he would have to turn his body and shift his feet before he went after you, and he wouldn't be able to do it fast enough to stop you. If you went around him too wide, he could turn his body as he moved and he could recover some of the time and get back into a good defensive position. I liked the wing drill, and I was good at it, too.

Coach set up a zigzag pattern of guys, and we had to dribble past them, always staying inside their elbows. We ran the drill a few times, and I saw Tomas move his elbow into guys as he drove and almost knock two of them down. They complained, but Coach just made some stupid remark about being men. I knew if Tomas did that in a game, somebody would knock his head off.

When Tomas went on defense, Sky gave him a shot and Ruffy hit him in the ribs, making him wince.

"Williams, sit down!" House again.

Okay, we all dug it. Nobody was supposed to touch Tomas. Just let him have his way.

We ran a light five-on-five, and I saw that the guys were checking out Tomas. Sky put some moves on him and he went for them. I got inside with him and called for the ball.

"Yo, Tomas, I'm going straight up," I said.

When the ball came into me, I took one dribble and went up. Tomas had his hands up but he hardly got off the floor. I made the easy shot over him. I heard the whistle and turned to see House signaling that I had walked.

"No way!" I called to him.

House knew I hadn't walked. Tomas knew it, too.

We finished practice with a passing drill that was a major snap because everybody wanted to show off their stuff. House kept yelling at us to get serious, but nobody was going there except Colin. Even

Tomas tried a little blind pass.

By the time we had showered and dressed, I was in a good mood. Ball did that for me. It was a warm day, and Ruffy and I bought some sodas from a guy with a cart on the way home.

"House is steady scoping you," Ruffy said. "He's looking for you to blow."

"Yeah, I'm hip," I said. "But to tell you the truth, I don't even care, man. If House wants to mess the team up, it's on him."

"How come you're not downtown?" Jocelyn said. "I thought you were going to help Mom with the shopping."

"Why didn't you call and remind me?"

"I'm not your secretary!"

Mom shopped on Ninth Avenue, across from her job at the Port Authority, on paydays. She had asked me to come down and take the stuff home. The whole thing with Tomas was so heavy on my mind, I had completely blown it. But I wasn't supposed to be there until four and it was just three thirty, so I was still cool.

I grabbed a gypsy cab on the avenue, whizzed

downtown for a big six dollars, and got to 41st and Ninth in a flash. Then I went up to the office my mom worked in and got introduced to all the people I had met a hundred thousand times before.

"You should apply for a job with the Port Authority police," a short, red-faced man said. "They're looking for more African Americans to join the force."

"Yeah, maybe I will," I said.

Mom started running down this whole rap about how the Port Authority staff was now going to be involved in feeding the hungry.

"And most of the program is due to your mother's initiative," Red-Face said.

They had collected six cartons of cold cuts, chips, and soda from neighborhood merchants, and me, Mom, and this Spanish woman named Sherry were going to give them out across the street at a homeless center. A porter from the Port Authority put all the stuff on a skid, and we went across the street.

This place was mostly a big room where people sat and played cards, ate, or got help filling out forms for different programs. I had seen it before because I always passed it when me and Mom went shopping on 41st.

Mom and Sherry wanted me to help give out food, but I wasn't down for it. So I just sat at one of the tables while they made the distribution.

"So who you?" This brother sat across from me at the table. He was definitely smelling funky, and his hair looked like he hadn't combed it in a serious while.

"Drew," I said, holding out my hand. "Drew Lawson. My mom is handing out the stuff we brought over."

"Where you live?"

"Uptown."

"So you one of them uptown folks thinking you better than everybody, huh?"

"Why you got to go there?" I said. "You don't know me."

"You know what I got in me?" he asked, pointing to his chest. "I got the truth."

"Yo, that's all good," I said.

"And the truth is that they don't care what you do, or what happens to you," he said. "That's why I'm homeless."

"Sorry to hear that, my man."

"Nah, man, you ain't sorry." The guy turned and started sniffing, and at first I thought he was crying, but then I saw he was just sniffing. That was funny to me, but I didn't want to bust a grin on my man.

"So where you from?" I asked.

"So where is *Mr. Ferguson* from?" he said.

"So where you from, *Mr. Ferguson*?"

"I'm from Chicago, and I came to New York because I wanted to bring truth to the people," he said. "But you know what? When I found out the real truth, I knew the people didn't want to hear it!"

"What's the real truth?" I asked.

"That don't nobody care if you homeless," he said. "Ain't nobody care if you laying dead in the street. Ain't nobody care if you ain't got nothing to eat."

"Yo, man, that's my mom over there bringing food and stuff to you people," I said. "She cares or she wouldn't be bringing it."

"No, man, she cares because she's homeless, too," Mr. Ferguson said. "She knows that anything she got from the Man can be taken back by the Man. And if the Man can mess with you like that, you ain't got nothing. You know what I mean?"

"Yeah," I lied.

"That's why I ain't putting myself out there in the Man's game," he said. "If you know you don't have a win, then there's no use for you being in the game. Ain't that right?"

"Not really."

"They got you brainwashed," he said, turning halfway around on the bench and talking over his shoulder. "They can't brainwash me because I been around. You ain't been nowhere."

"Yeah, right."

"I guess you okay," he said. "But I ain't sure. You sound too *white* to me."

The guy was still smelling funky, he was talking stupid, and I was getting the feeling that I might be getting bugs on me or something. I waited with Mom while she finished handing out the food. What I saw was that most of the people didn't care if they got food or not. One old man was complaining that diet soda caused cancer and we shouldn't be handing them out to people. When he said that, Mr. Ferguson jumped right in about how cancer was the government's secret way of getting rid of people it didn't want.

As we were leaving, Mr. Ferguson called out that he bet I was glad I was leaving. He was right.

Me and Mom went to the meat market between 41st and 42nd and bought umpteen pounds of hamburger, some chicken, sausages, and large cans of black beans. All the time, she was thanking God about having a job and a decent place to live and how I should be thankful, too.

"You see them poor people over there?" she said. "People should come see them and be thankful for what God has given them."

Mom had to go back to work for another hour, and I took the stuff uptown.

On the way I thought about Mr. Ferguson. I figured he had pickled his brain with cheap booze years ago, and maybe even drugs. But he was right about some things. I knew I really didn't care for the dude.

And I started thinking that probably nobody in his family cared for him, either. Or maybe if they cared, they couldn't deal with him being so off the wall. It amounted to about the same thing. But something he said bothered me. He said if you didn't have a win, you might as well give up and get out of the game. That was what he was doing—getting out of the game. But with him it was straight up. Maybe with some of the guys on the corner it was the same thing, but they just weren't dealing with it.

"So you and Mom save the world?" Jocelyn parked herself on the end of my bed and started painting her toenails.

"You staying on my bed all the time, people are going to be talking about incest," I said.

"You're not getting in anything, so between us it's going to be outcest and that's just another word for friendship," she came back. "Did you feel like Jesus feeding the multitudes?"

"I didn't like it," I said. "Mom was trying to get me into one of those good-doing moods or something."

"Why didn't you like it?"

"I saw some of the food they were giving out. It was plain stuff. White bread, beans, some hot dogs. If you were hungry, then it was better than nothing, but you got to leave your pride outside when you get on the food line. Mom said some of the folks down there were crackheads and that was the only food they got. I definitely saw some winos."

"I feel sorry for them," Jocelyn said.

"So why don't you go down there with Mom and feed them?"

"Because I don't like to see them," Jocelyn said. "You know, I was thinking about what they should do with their lives and whatnot."

"Yeah?"

"I didn't come up with anything too tough," Jocelyn said. "I'm thinking about painting my nails blue next time. What you think about blue?"

"You wear sneakers all the time, so nobody can see your stupid toes," I said. "What difference does the color make?"

"The kinds of jobs they need don't even exist anymore. We went over that in social studies. To get a decent job, you need a decent education."

"Now you sound like Dr. Barker."

"Well, he might be a fool, but he's still right," Jocelyn said, standing up and looking down at her toes. "If you can't do nothing, you got to take what they give you. You want to carry me to my room so I won't smudge my nails?"

"You've been reading about those African queens again?"

"I do think I look like Nefertiti." Jocelyn turned her profile toward me. "What you think?"

"Just like her, Jocelyn," I said. "You look just like her."

I watched as my sister put on her queenly walk and left the room.

What she said made sense. I couldn't see Mr. Ferguson holding down a regular job. None of the men and women I saw in that center looked like they were ready for prime time. I could see them all copping a plea and shuffling to the back of the bus.

I thought of what Mr. Ferguson had said about not playing the game if you didn't have a win. But he was living too funky to be throwing that jive down for some wisdom.

But it wasn't just the ones I saw downtown who weren't playing the game. There were a whole lot of brothers I couldn't imagine making a real getover. Some of them had been on the corner for so long, it looked like they were supposed to be there.

I got up and went to Jocelyn's door. It was open and she was sitting at the computer.

"Hey, Nefertiti, why don't you want to see those

homeless people downtown?" I asked her.

"For the same reason I don't want to see any dead people," Jocelyn answered. "I don't want to see nothing that looks anything like me messed up like that."

"I'm hip to that."

Jocelyn was doing her homework, and I went back to my room and took out my books. My mind wasn't on the books, though. It was on House and Tomas. What I thought was that House was messing with me, and I was going to back off and let it slide until the team started losing, and then House would have to come to me and my game. But if Tomas could pull the team around him, or if House just let the team lose, then I would be out of it without even being in the game. I would be doing the same sitting-out shuffle that Ferguson was. I had to come up with my B plan.

Morning. I went out to the kitchen and my folks were having an argument about who forgot to play the lottery. My father said that my mother was supposed to put his numbers in, and she said that if he wanted to play, he should have put his own numbers in.

"I asked you to do it, woman!" he said, standing in the doorway. "If you weren't going to put my numbers in, you should have said something."

"They didn't come out anyway," Mom said. "So what are you worried about?"

Mom got her handbag and kissed Jocelyn on the forehead and me on the side of the head, and they went out the door arguing. I was going to say something to Jocelyn about how stupid I thought playing the lottery was, but I didn't want to get her started on odds and stuff.

"How come you're late getting up today?" she asked.

"Who died and made you the head of the FBI?"

"How did your practice go yesterday?"

"Why?"

"So do you think the United States should be more aggressive in its trade policies?" she went on. "I'll be on the phone to the president this afternoon, so if I could get your input now . . ."

"What were they arguing about?" I asked.

"He doesn't have any money and she won't give him any," she said. "You know that's going to go on until they catch up on the bills."

"Yeah, I guess." With my family it was always catching up on the bills or explaining to the electric company why we hadn't sent the payment in. My folks didn't mess up their money; it was just that they weren't making that much to begin with.

"I imagine I'll have to start my modeling career early to support you people." Jocelyn licked some of the jelly off a piece of toast. "But don't worry about it. I'm big that way."

I got to school a minute late, and Mr. Harrison, who was on desk duty, looked the other way as I slid past the desk and into the stairwell.

In English I sat down next to Sandy Harris, a thin, brown-skinned girl with eyes the same color as her skin and a low, kind of sexy voice. We got into another discussion about *Othello* and I noticed that a lot of the kids were saying it wasn't about race. I still wasn't going for it, and I said so.

"Iago didn't like the brother being a big-time general and he didn't like him getting over with a big-time white chick, either," I said. "And since he was white like everybody else around at the time, he had the power to mess with Othello."

"Is it really the woman? Or the celebrity that Othello's achieved?" Miss Tomita asked. "We do know that Iago hoped for high office."

"I don't know," I said.

"And doesn't that make the play interesting?"

"So what's the answer?" I asked.

"Well, since Shakespeare isn't around to answer our questions, it depends on our interpretations, doesn't it?" Miss Tomita said.

I didn't exactly understand what she meant by that, but I could tell she was happy with it.

I could see myself as Othello, a kick-butt general who had climbed to the top and had to deal with Iago and all the other suckies around him. Desdemona, his old lady, was like a symbol of what he had achieved in his life, and Iago was messing with it. He was saying that Desdemona wasn't really happening for him, that his dream of her was messed up. I could see how that could turn a brother's head inside out.

What I figured was that as long as it was me doing my thing, a black player on a black team, then it would be about me and the team. If House could get Tomas in the spotlight instead of me, it was going to be about him and Tomas. What I had to do was outplay Tomas every time I stepped on the court. He couldn't put Tomas in the headlines when my game was blowing up in all the stats.

Our next league game was against Frederick Douglass Academy. House ran down this lame rap about how this game was going to show our character and whatnot. He said that we should be able to beat FDA if we played our game. FDA was one of those schools that never had a real big-time player but always had enough going on to mess with you if you showed weak. Every year some team waltzed over to 148th Street looking for an easy jam only to come slinking away with a loss.

FDA plays a two-one-two shallow zone most of the time. Their guards play close to the three-point line, their center plays about two feet closer to the basket than most, and their forwards are in tight, too. They cut off penetration but give up a lot of three-point shots.

House had Ernie at guard, Ruffy at center, and Sky and Tomas at forward. I thought that was lame from the get-go, because Tomas should have earned his starting position, not just had it handed to him. He hadn't dominated anybody in the one game he had played with us and wasn't kicking any butt at practice, either.

FDA was up for the game, especially on defense, but their offense was weak and the game began slowly. We were up by five after a few minutes, and I thought it was going to be easy but they hung on, and then, with the slow pace, they caught up and it was back and forth. At the end of the first quarter it was 14–14. On offense we were trying to pick off their forwards and set up backdoor plays, but they were playing too tight to get that going. We were running into ourselves and just turning the ball over on the inside. Plus Ruffy had two fouls already.

I think FDA thought they were going to lose before the game, but when they saw they were playing us even, they began to pick up the pace.

If a team is revving up the tempo, you have to react quickly or they might get a momentum thing going on and you can't catch them. FDA ran two fast breaks in a row at the start of the second quarter, one off a rebound and the other off a turnover when Tomas held the ball too low and their guard came back and slapped it loose. The next time we came down, I saw their guards edging away from their zones, looking for another fast break. Colin was in for Ernie and called for the two-swing play. That's when both guards move to the right, the center comes out, and the right forward goes backdoor. The guard with the ball passes out to the center, who passes in to the forward, who is free because the other forward has picked his man in the low post. If the low pick doesn't work, then the forward comes out and the right side of the zone is overloaded. Colin was going to pass out to Ruffy but got tied up and passed it to me, and I was free. The FDA forward lost his man and picked his own teammate looking for him, which left the lane open.

I went hard, and nobody even came near to me as I scored the deuce. The same dude on FDA who had lost his man took the ball out and made a weak pass that was supposed to go over my head at the foul line. I grabbed it and went right back inside, got the deuce, and was fouled. Then I nailed the free throw.

FDA came down again, their shooting guard threw up something that looked like half an alley-oop, and Ruffy got it and flung the sucker downcourt. Tomas was down with me on a two-against-one. Their center wasn't that tall but he was quick. I had the ball at the foul line as Tomas slid away toward the basket. I thought their center might switch when I faked the handoff to Tomas. He didn't and came after me as I started the shot.

All I saw was this big palm over my head. I floated the ball over him and it went in. We were up by four and FDA called a time-out.

"That was a prayer and you know it!" The FDA player looked like he was pissed. I liked that.

"If you had a game, you would have stopped it," I said.

During the time-out House told Ricky to go in for me. I shot him a look and he was glowering.

"What's wrong with you, man?" I asked him.

"You are," he said. "Now sit down and watch the game. Maybe you'll learn something."

"What you mean, *learn* something?" I asked.

House turned away.

At halftime we had managed to get up by seven, but FDA was still in the game and Ruffy had picked up another foul. We still had the win as far as I was concerned. All we needed to do was take it. But as soon as we hit the locker room at halftime, House opened up on me.

"Drew, you're playing for yourself, not the team!" he said. "We're trying to get a team effort out there, and you're going out for showtime at the Apollo. I don't need this crap and the team doesn't need it."

I knew I wasn't going to start the second half, but I thought I would play. FDA kept the game close all the way. Our team kept looking over at the bench, waiting for the coach to send me back in. Our guys were playing good, but they weren't playing strong. FDA got solid and had caught up with three minutes on the clock.

"Yo, House, put me in, man." I was mad at myself for even asking him.

He didn't answer, just turned away.

With a minute to go in the game, FDA went up by five. Ernie and Colin were at guards, and FDA, smelling a chance for a win, were all over them. Ruffy got a deuce to cut it to three. We got a turnover when the refs called a three-second violation on their big man. Sky came down the sideline and threw up a jumper from just inside the three-point line and we were down by one. FDA tried to freeze the ball, but they got too careful and lost it again on a close-guarding call with ten seconds to go. We had a time-out left and House called it.

"We want to get the ball down in a hurry and set up something off the penetration," he said. "Ruffy, your man is laying off. You come out and set a pick in the middle of the lane. Ricky brings the ball left to right and looks for the pass at the top of the key.

Colin goes in the opposite direction through the lane. Sky sets a pick for Tomas. Ricky, it's up to you to see who's free. If nobody's free, you take the shot and everybody hits the boards. On three! One! Two! Three!"

My whole body was jumping, I wanted to be in so bad. Mad and hurt at the same time, I couldn't believe that House was being so stupid. We had been running picks all day, so I knew they were looking for them. Colin inbounded the ball to Ricky and went to the far side. Ricky dribbled to the side of the key, and I knew it was taking too long. Tomas got in front of his man off the pick five feet from the hoop and Ricky fired the ball to him. But instead of taking it right up, he put the ball on the floor once, tried a fake, and then went up.

The FDA forward went up with him. He got the ball on the rise and slapped it toward midcourt. Ricky went after it, catching it just before it went out-of-bounds as the buzzer sounded. The game was over.

"Why did you pull up?" Sky was all over Tomas. "You should have gone in and jammed! If you didn't make it, the sucker would have had to foul you. Why you throwing up some *pussy* shot, man?"

Sky was right. Tomas should have taken the ball inside and attacked the rim. But it wasn't all his fault.

"We shouldn't have been behind in the first place," I said. "I should have had that ball, and everybody knows it!"

"Watch your mouth, Drew!" House yelled at me.

"Why I got to watch my mouth?" I asked. "We shouldn't have lost this game and you know it."

I was fuming. House took a step toward me, and Fletch stepped in front of him. I wished the sucker had stepped to me. I was ready to knock him out.

"I think House was betting on the game," Ricky called out.

"That had better be a joke," House barked at him.

"You see anybody laughing?" Ricky asked.

"We could have won with me in there!" I said. "And everybody here knows that!"

"I don't know it!" House was shouting. "And I'm the coach."

"Well, you're the only one who don't know it," Ruffy said.

"Look, I can replace this whole team if I have to," House said.

"With dudes who like to lose, I guess," Ruffy said.

House told Ruffy to meet him in his office in the morning. Ruffy said no and he meant it.

Outside, it was cold and there was a light rain. I watched some of the FDA players laughing and joking as they walked down the street. Just the way they were feeling good, I was feeling bad.

Ruffy hailed a gypsy cab because he had to go see his brother's lawyer. As he got into the cab, I told him I'd call him later.

"Hey, Drew, which way you going?" It was Tomas.

"Down the way," I said, nodding downtown.

"Can I walk with you?"

"Yeah, I guess."

We walked down the hill without talking. I knew he wanted me to let him off the hook about losing the game, but he didn't know how to say it.

"I don't like losing," he said finally.

"Nobody does."

"Why didn't you play the second half?" he asked.

"House has his game going and he's the coach," I said. "Anything I do is counterfeit, I guess."

"I wish you had played," he said.

"Yeah, well, that's the way it goes," I said.

I didn't want to deal with Tomas. I didn't trust him. Maybe he was just coming over to see what I was thinking. I imagined him calling House and telling him what I said.

"You think I lost the game?" he asked.

"The team lost the game," I said. "The coach, everybody. You did your part, too."

"You know I want to play basketball the same as you." Tomas spoke softly. "In Europe a lot of boys want to come to America and play ball. We see the American players with their big cars and big houses and they're all smiling when they look at you on television. We want to wear the same clothes and get money to wear the different brands. We want that, too. There's no difference in what is in my heart and what is in your heart."

"Yeah, but you came over here and you're starting on the team," I said. "If I went to your school, would I be starting?"

"Sure you would." He grinned. "Everybody in Europe thinks that black people are like gods. They think you don't jump—you fly."

"In my case it's true," I said.

"Drew, I'm sorry we lost."

"Yeah, I'll see you tomorrow," I said.

Tomas left me at the corner with a little wave.

Going home, I was thinking about Tomas, what he said about things not being different between his life and mine. Maybe they had a high opinion of black ballplayers in Prague, but we were in America, and what I had to deal with was where I was. Just like my man Othello had to deal with where he was.

What I was wondering was whether or not House would let us go on losing games to make his point.

got all the numbers you asked for," Jocelyn said when I got home. She was drying her nails.

"What numbers?"

"About who's going to win basketball games," she said. "The teams with the highest percentage of their baskets on layups win more times than teams with the lowest percentage of their baskets on layups."

"Yeah, but who's scoring the layups?" I asked. "It could be the guards."

"It doesn't matter," Jocelyn said. "The percentages always work out. I checked it out with the

NBA, and they agree with me."

"You called the NBA?"

"I might even apply for a job with them over the summer," she said. "Although as cute as I am, I could be a distraction to their players."

"What did you say, girl?" Mom had come into the kitchen in her housecoat. "As *cute* as you are?"

"Mama, you know I'm fine." Jocelyn flashed Mom a smile over her shoulder.

"Well, nobody is going to accuse you of being too modest, that's for sure," Mom said.

"Actually, I see my beauty as a handicap, a burden I have to tolerate and which threatens to cover up my great intellect," Jocelyn said.

"Did you tell Drew that Ruffy called?" Mom was peeling onions.

"What did he say?" I asked.

"They have some pretrial stuff going on tomorrow, and he wants you to go down there with him to the court," Jocelyn said. "He said his mama can't make it because she has to go to a doctor's appointment. She's probably stressed out. I told him you probably wouldn't go to court since your picture was put up in the post office."

"Yo, I think I should go," I said. "I can tell them I'm a relative."

"Will you be missing anything important in school?" Mom asked.

"Nothing I can't make up," I said.

"You know, I feel so bad about Tony," Mama said, ignoring Mouth Almighty. "I always loved that boy."

"Everybody loved him," Jocelyn said. "He still messed up. I was talking to Bianca, and she said that Tony's mother is so upset, she can't sleep or anything. That's why she can't go to court to find out what's going on. Tony's mother said when she went to see him downtown and saw him in his prison clothes, she just broke down on the spot. She's the one we need to feel sorry for."

"A lot of our young men mess up, Jocelyn," Mom said. "But if we don't support them, who's going to raise the next generation of black children?"

"I'm waiting for the UFOs to land so I can marry a Martian," Jocelyn said. "And I hope he has some money when he gets here."

I thought Jocelyn could have shown a little more feeling for Tony than she did, but she was right.

Tony had messed up. But for some reason, it didn't sound like such a big deal. It was almost like—Hey, that's the way we live in the hood, and getting caught is just part of the routine. Mom okayed me going to the pretrial, and I met Ruffy at the corner of 145th, down from the bus garage. We took the 3 train downtown. Ruffy was wearing his suit, and he had brought a pad to take notes. The train got crowded at 96th Street and stayed that way until we reached 14th.

I had my fake ID saying I was nineteen, but we didn't even need it. Ruffy had the name of the judge, and we found the right courtroom on the seventh floor.

The courtroom was nearly empty except for people at the three tables in the front. Tony, in his orange jumpsuit, sat with his lawyer at one of them.

A policewoman was talking when Ruffy and I got there. She was saying that she had checked in the guns when they were brought into the police station.

"And are those the weapons lying on the desk in front of the clerk?" A tall, thin man in a brown suit pointed to the guns.

Before the woman could answer, Tony's lawyer started objecting, but the judge held up his hand and said that he would let the guns be brought in as evidence. Then the woman said she would have to see the tags, and she was shown the tags and then she said they were the same weapons that she had checked in.

Tony looked back and saw Ruffy and me sitting there. Ruffy nodded and Tony nodded back. The judge looked over to where we sat, and so did one of the officers in the front of the room. We weren't sitting too near the front and nobody looked nervous.

The case went on. It wasn't like television. Nobody seemed excited. In fact, it looked like everybody was bored. I tried to check out the other two defendants, but they mostly kept their heads down.

Ruffy and I didn't speak while the hearing was going on, but when there was a break, he asked me if I knew them.

"No," I said.

"That's Norman and Little G," Ruffy said. "Remember them from Marcus Garvey Park?"

"Oh, yeah."

Norman and Little G used to play ball with the older guys, but neither one of them really had any serious game. Norman had got a girl pregnant and tried to make her get rid of it, and the girl had been crippled. That was all I knew about him except that both he and Little G were losers nobody liked and everybody was half afraid of because they were always into something dangerous.

At noon the hearing ended for the day. After Tony had been taken away, his lawyer came over to us and said he was glad we could make it.

"When the actual trial starts, we want the jury to see that Tony has a family. That way they're more likely to think of him as a human being rather than just a felon," he said. "Is your mother coming tomorrow?"

"I think so," Ruffy said.

"It'll help if she can make it," the lawyer said.

We went into the hallway, and Ruffy called his mom to tell her the hearing was over for the day. I looked at everybody wandering around in the hall. Mostly young black men I figured were on trial or going to see them except for a fine-looking Latina sister in handcuffs. I gave her a smile and she looked away. It wasn't smiling time.

We got on the elevator, and there was an older brother already in the car. He had real wide shoulders but he kept them hunched forward. He was leaning over and trying to catch his breath. I thought he might be having a heart attack.

"Yo, you okay?" I asked.

"Not guilty," he said, looking up at me. "I'm walking, man. I'm walking."

"Yeah, that's all good," I said.

When we left the building, the guy stopped and took a deep breath. I didn't know what had happened with him, but I could see he was glad to be free and out in the world.

The court scene got me down. I thought about what Jocelyn had said, that Tony had messed up even though people loved him. Maybe being loved wasn't enough; maybe there was something else you needed not to get in trouble. Then I thought about the older guy in the elevator. He was walking out of the building, but it must have been a close call because he was still shaking.

"That guy was still trying to catch his breath," I said to Ruffy as we started walking uptown.

"So am I," Ruffy said.

I looked at him and he wasn't smiling.

At practice House set up backdoor plays over and over, with one of the forwards sliding off center picks for the bucket. Everybody on the team knew he was setting stuff up for Tomas, but we didn't kick it around. All during practice I was watching the guys, seeing if they were on my side or slipping over to Tomas. I didn't want to be suspicious of them, but that was the way I was feeling. I knew I could trust Ruffy, but I wasn't sure about the others.

We also practiced maintaining distances, because the guys were bunching up too much, especially when we were trying to overload a zone defense.

After practice I walked home with Ruffy and we talked about what colleges we wanted to go to.

"I just want to go to a school where if you're wearing their name on your jacket, people are going to know who you're talking about," I said. "A guy I know went to Bethany College out in Kansas. People kept asking him where it was and if it was a real school, so he stopped wearing their jacket."

"I want to go to a school where all the girls have big legs," Ruffy said. "And it's okay if they're not too smart, too."

"Yo, man, that's wrong," I said.

"You know, Tony's lawyer can still cop a plea if he wants," Ruffy said. "If he cops, he'll get three to five."

"If he doesn't cop?"

"They got about seven charges. The max looks like fifteen years."

A fifteen-year bid is too cold to even think about. We didn't talk any more on the way home.

It was just before lunch, and me, Ricky, and our boy Domingo were sitting in the media center trying to find his house on the website where you can locate areas from a satellite. While we looked, we were also running down our viewpoints about girls, because Ricky had some funny ideas.

"The reason Puerto Rican girls are the best-looking is that we got the best mixture," Ricky said. "We got African blood, Spanish blood, and just the right mixture of Taino, which is Indian. That's what gives Puerto Rican mamas that delicate look."

"They look delicate, but they can't touch girls

from the Dominican Republic, because our girls are deep, and when you see a girl from the DR, all of that comes right through her eyes," Domingo said. "You can even ask Drew, and he's not from the DR."

"Ask me?" I looked at Domingo to see if he was serious and saw that he was. "I've never said anything about girls from the DR being so fine."

"Yeah, but you're honest, man," Domingo said. Just as he was talking, Colin came over and sat down at our table.

"That my neighborhood!" Ricky pointed to the computer screen.

We tried to home in on his house, but he couldn't recognize the streets from the top view. Then he wanted to switch to this girl's house he was trying to get next to.

"See if we can find her house, and then I'll tell her I used to live over there," Ricky said.

"Yo, Colin, who do you think are the best-looking"—Domingo held his hands up like he was settling something serious—"Puerto Rican girls or Dominican girls?"

"How come black girls aren't in there?" I asked.

"I think Irish girls are the best-looking," Colin said.

"Yo, he got to say that," Ricky cracked. "My man is trying to hold up his peeps. But show me one Irish girl in this school who's really smoking!"

"There aren't any Irish girls in this school," Colin said.

"That's because they can't stand the competition!" Ricky said.

That was stupid, but I liked it anyway. We messed around some more, dissing each other's women until the period ended. Me and Domingo started out toward the lunchroom, Ricky had to go and get another battery for his cell, and Colin was rapping with the media teacher. House saw me in the hall and came over.

"Hey, Drew, you headed for lunch?"

"Yeah."

"Come on, I'll treat you to some decent food," he said. "We can go to Tacky's."

Tacky's was the name everybody gave to La Taqueria, a Mexican restaurant that had just opened in the hood. It looked kind of expensive, so I had never eaten there, but some of the teachers talked about it like it was special.

When House asked me if I wanted to have lunch with him, I froze a little. We had been avoiding each other most of the time and I didn't know what to expect. But I don't back down, so I said okay.

The restaurant was only two blocks away, and on the way over he was talking about how the neighborhood was improving.

"Five years ago you couldn't walk around here for all the crackheads," he said. "And in the evenings I used to worry about the players getting home safe."

"Yeah, well, things change," I said, knowing how lame I sounded.

The thing was that I didn't like House, but I knew I had to get along with him because that was the way things were, as Fletch said. House was the coach and I was the player. So I was running up my little truce flag and I guessed he was running up his, but I still knew what I was going to do when I got on the court, and he wasn't going to change that.

The inside of La Taqueria was sharp. They had photographs on the wall of these old-time Mexican dudes with belts of ammunition around their chests and pistols in their belts. All the tables were dark wood with red-and-white place mats. I thought Jocelyn would have dug it.

House ordered chicken enchiladas, salad, and rice, and I got tacos, refried beans, and salad. We also ordered iced tea.

"So how are things going?" House asked me.

"Okay, I guess," I said.

"You looking forward to the Warrick game?"

"I look forward to every game," I said.

The waitress brought the iced tea, and House dumped sugar in it without even tasting it. I tasted mine and it was already sweetened. I figured the dude was nervous.

"You looking forward to the game?" I asked House.

"I am," he said, "but I was kind of puzzled about the way the team dynamics seem to be shaping up."

"What's that supposed to mean?"

"You seem to be unhappy about something," he said.

"Yeah, well, you know, you're changing the way we play," I said. "We were doing all right during the first half of the season, and we did all right last year. I don't see why we're changing now."

"Why do you think we're changing?" House was sipping his tea, and I knew it had to be too sweet.

"I don't know," I said.

"Hey, you're a man, I'm a man," House said. "If you have something to say, you should spit it out."

What I figured was that he wanted to have it out with me. I was going to be cool with it, lay it out careful, but I didn't like that "you're a man" stuff.

"Yeah, okay—look, as soon as Tomas and Colin showed up, you started running the team around them," I said. "Everybody sees it. The whole team is talking about it, even Tomas—but you keep running into your office like you don't hear it. You want to get to square business, then you know the same thing I do."

House leaned back in his chair and looked around the restaurant. There were a few other customers, and the waiters were setting up their tables.

"You know what surprises me, Drew?" House turned back to me. "What surprises me is that you think you're pushing yourself. You think that you're out there trying your best to win because it's the best thing for the team, right?"

"Yeah."

"But do you know what every college coach asks me about every good black player who comes along?" House spoke softly. "He asks me if the player can be coached. In other words, can he fit into a college system. When I asked Fletch what he thought of your game . . ."

"Yeah, what did he say?"

"He said he didn't want to talk about it that much," House said. "But he did say you were a really good individual player. I got the feeling that he doesn't think you can fit into a team plan."

The waitress brought the food and set it down. It smelled good. The busboy brought over a tray with little cups of sauces and a bowl of chips.

"Fletch said that?" I asked.

"Not in so many words," House said. "But word gets around to the scouts. You know what I mean?"

"The way you're sounding is like I shouldn't put too much faith in my game," I said.

"I'm not saying that you shouldn't believe in your game, but I am saying that you need to look over your shoulder once in a while, too."

The food suddenly didn't look too good. We talked a little more, mostly light stuff about school and what was going on in the world, but my heart wasn't in it. The dude had left me when he talked smack about my game. I was glad when he paid the bill and gladder still to watch him walk away toward the office when we were back in school.

I have never ever liked anybody who went to Warrick High for the Arts. They were all working too hard at being different. But Warrick was in our division, and they could always get somebody on the court who could play ball. They had one skinny white dude who could shoot the eyes out of the basket. Ruffy said it was the same guy every year.

"They keep him down in the basement. One year they'll throw a few freckles on him, and the next year they'll change the color of his hair or mess with his eyebrows, but it's the same dude."

The way to stop dudes like that was to muscle

them. Go to a man-to-man on offense, back them into the paint, and score underneath. Then just beat them to death on defense. Don't let them play their game, or they would weird out the gym and leave you looking stupid.

We had already lost to FDA, and Warrick was not supposed to be a powerhouse. A loss to them would put the whole regular season in retard gear.

We got to Warrick and they had their freaky-looking cheerleaders—four white girls, two sisters, and an Asian girl—out front waiting for our bus. They all had red hair, dark makeup that was two seconds from goth, and about a yard of attitude.

What they had different this year was this big cornbread brother at center.

We warmed up and I tried to be cool, but I could feel myself getting worked up. House never wanted us to look at the team we were going to play, but all of us kept sneaking looks over at Warrick and the new guy everybody was talking about at center. He looked strong, black, and ready. Dude had the longest arms I had ever seen on a human being.

"He's listed at six-eleven," Colin said. "I think he's seven feet easy."

Abdul said he played against him in Marcus Garvey Park. "He's strong," Abdul said. "Plus he's funky smelling. I don't think the guy ever washes."

"He got any moves?" I asked.

"Nothing, but when he backed into me, his butt was in my chest," Abdul said. "That's a funny feeling, man. Some dude is bent over and backing his butt into your chest."

The one-minute buzzer went off, and House called us together. "This is a slow team," he said. "They rely on rebounding and set plays. We're going to have to box out on the boards big-time, and make our plays on offense. We can't win a shootout with these guys unless we out-rebound them, and with this guy Tyrone Scott at center, I don't think that's going to happen. Ruffy, you have to do your best to keep him off the boards. Tomas and Sky need to help out when they can. Colin and Ricky need to stay on top of their guards. Anybody coming off the bench needs to remember we're trying to play team ball. Okay, put your hands together."

I put my hand out, but the set was stinking up the place. I wasn't starting.

Ruffy came over to me and put his arm around me.

"Hey, you ain't starting, I ain't playing," he said.

"No, don't let him take our game," I said. "You go on and start. Give me some time to think it through."

"Whatever you say, and whenever you say it, I got your back, Drew." Me and Ruffy slapped hands, and he turned to go out to the center of the court.

I felt like pure D crap. I didn't think any of the regular team wanted to see me sitting. But I wasn't sure.

Fletch sat next to me on the bench. "How deep is your game?" he asked.

"It's deep enough to—" I turned to answer him and he held his hand up. "Why you ask?"

"Just something you need to be thinking about," he said. "I'm glad to see you keeping your cool. If somebody is trying to take something from you because it makes them feel good to play with your head, the best answer is a smile. You know what I'm saying?"

I didn't know what he meant and I wasn't keeping my cool. I could feel the tears coming, or wanting to come, and nothing Fletch said would change that. Plus I was thinking about what House had said in Tacky's and wondering if Fletch was playing mind games with me.

The game started with the jump ball. Ruffy couldn't get up anywhere near Scott, and they controlled the tap. I knew the brother bringing the ball down—Marquis Webb. He was tough but short. He brought the ball down, and all the time Ruffy was fighting in the center. Their big man was doing a swim movement on Ruffy, using his arms to get in front of him while using his feet to back him in. The way he moved, with his legs apart and slow, I figured he was going to be the kind of player who parked in the lane and stayed there all day unless the refs came up with some three-second violations.

Ruffy was trying to keep him out, but Scott backed in deep enough so when the ball came in, he could just turn and muscle up a deuce.

Colin brought the ball down for us, and House was already calling out a play from the sidelines. I thought that was lame because the team hadn't even got into the flow yet. Sky and Tomas tried a switch pick and Scott ran into it, but Sky got boxed in and

Colin threw the ball away.

Warrick came down again and Marquis brought it inside fast to Scott, who whipped it out to the white guard, number 14. I swear that fool was going up even before it reached his hands. He went straight up, brought the right elbow into a perfect line with the hoop, and let go a beautiful arc. Ricky watched it as he boxed him out, but he didn't need to because that ball didn't touch anything but net.

Ruffy looked over at me. We both knew that number 14 was their shooter. Colin brought the ball down again and passed it in to Ruffy. Ruffy tried a hook and Scott slapped it away. Ricky got the loose ball, put a move on number 14, and went around him. Scott stepped out, and when Ricky went for the dunk, Scott had both hands on the ball. The home crowd started screaming as Scott wagged his finger at Ricky.

The whole first quarter was the Scott show, with his knocking away our shots and snatching bounds with one hand. But it was their number 14 who hit three threes and a layup to lift them to a 20–9 first-quarter lead.

House put in Ernie Alvarez for Ricky, but I knew

it wasn't going to make a difference. We were still running set plays, and the guys looked like they didn't know what they were doing.

During the second quarter Ruffy was forcing Scott farther and farther out. It was strength against strength, and Ruffy was out-muscling their big man. When Scott started complaining to the ref that he was being pushed, I figured we had a chance. But number 14 hit three more threes, and at the half they had us 37–22. Fifteen points was hard to overcome against anybody, but it was really hard against a big man who had picked up only two fouls in the first half.

They had a scoreboard with all the players listed. I saw that Tomas had scored two points.

On the way to the locker room Fletch touched my arm. I asked him how come I still wasn't playing.

"House thought it was going to be an easy game. That Scott didn't do anything against Bryant," Fletch said. "We lose this game, you might lose your season."

"Yo, man, you sound like you putting it on me," I said.

"Does it sound that way?" Fletch asked.

Fletch walked away, and I just felt like all of a sudden I was carrying a truck on my back. I felt so tired. It was like my whole life was spinning around me and I wasn't digging on any of it.

"We're not playing sharp ball out there," House said. "We're leaving the perimeter open for the three, and we're not getting enough offensive rebounds."

"Hey, coach, we're not leaving that dude open." Ricky spoke up. "He gets the ball off so fast, you can't get it. He knows he's going to shoot when he's getting to a spot. He's not setting up, he's just all touch and burn."

"He's getting too many open shots," House said. "I can count them and I can see when they're coming up. You're out there on the floor—you should see it, too."

I was down as we warmed up for the second half, but then Fletch came over and told me I was going to start.

"How come?"

"Why do you care?" he asked. "You don't want to play?"

"Yeah, I want to play," I said. "What'd you mean, if we lose today my season might be lost?"

"You can't lose more than two games and hope to get into the playoffs," Fletcher said. "And we haven't played against Boogie yet. Not in a real game."

I wanted to say something about what House had run down in the restaurant, about how my game wasn't going to make it for me, but at the same time I didn't. It was like saying that your mind was someplace else because your old lady was messing around and didn't love you anymore. I wanted to believe in my game, no matter what anybody else said, or what doubts I had.

I was excited to walk out on the court. Number 14 was kneeling, pulling up his socks, when I got to him.

"Hey, white boy, I'm going to eat you up this half."

"Hey, black boy," he said, standing, "how come I'm the one with the knife and fork and you didn't even start the game?"

Yeah. Right. I was ready. The ball went up and Scott slapped it toward their backcourt, but Ricky, who was starting with me, cut across and picked it off. I took off for the hoop and Ricky let the pass go just right. The ball bounced ahead of me just inside the foul line, I got it on the rise, and went up for my first deuce of the game.

The whole team came alive. We dogged Warrick into mistakes, and our fast break was kicking strong. In two minutes we had scored seven baskets to their one and were trailing by three when they copped a time-out.

"Let's keep the ball under control!" House said. "They're probably going to stay in a man-to-man defense, so we can work our inside plays deep. Drew, don't get wild on me!"

I looked away from House. He was still trying to get back to his weak plan. He made some more noises about us needing to be on the alert for transitions. That's what we had been all about when we were on the court, and he knew it. Fast breaks don't come out of thin air.

Warrick came out in a more settled way, slowing the game down. I knew they were still watching the scoreboard figuring to nurse their little lead. They backed Scott into Ruffy with their big man yelling at the refs that Ruffy was fouling him. Refs don't like that, so they called a three-second violation against him.

Ricky brought the ball down, and I saw they had switched to a two-two-one zone, daring us to go inside against Scott. I took up the challenge. Ricky picked 14 for me at the top of the key, which wasn't a big deal because he wasn't playing any real D. Their forward came over late, and I went by him right at Scott.

Scott was big, with long arms, but he must have been playing against chumps, because when I got to him he was standing straight up. No way he was going to have any leap, and I knew it as I took off over him. When I came down, he was looking up at the basket.

Their fans were oohing and aahing and I was feeling good. If I had been in the playground, I would have been talking, but I didn't want to say anything and draw a technical.

Ricky was getting the ball around, and at the end of the third quarter we were up by six and it looked like it was time for cruise control. They had the ball at the beginning of the fourth quarter, and number 14 brought it down slow. Ruffy was killing Scott in the pivot, and Tomas and Sky were rebounding tough. I went out toward 14 to stop the ball and saw him dip his knees and shift for a shot. He was fast on the gun, but I was faster in the air. But what he did was a high crossover and a quick step around me.

Twisting in the air, I reached for him and tried to get my first step going before I came down. I got my foot on the ground a half step behind 14 and was trying to plant my back foot when he cut across my path, making me stop so I wouldn't foul him, then brought the ball between his legs back outside.

When I turned, I was off-balance and stumbling and he was going up for a shot. I didn't even have to look to know he wasn't going to be touching anything but net. The dude had turned me completely around and almost had me on the floor.

That got their team going, and they staged a comeback with 14 leading the way. But we were holding on and playing well.

Tomas could work his man inside. He was playing against this brother who was deep into his game, moving and throwing elbows. He could get up high, but Tomas was controlling his space around the boards and coming up with his share of rebounds. He was hesitating on offense, but he was getting the ball out to me and Ricky.

I got this feeling that I was right where I wanted to be in the world. On the court, playing in a tough game, just as good as I needed to be. What was going to happen, who was going to win or lose, depended on who had the most heart, the most game. There were no numbers to worry about, no books to read, just me and what I knew: the court, the hoop, the sound of the ball on the floor.

"Yo, yo, Drew." The refs had called a time-out, and Ricky had my arm. "That white guy ain't got nothing but an outside shot. He's not going inside."

"He doesn't have anything but that one shot and the moves to get open, but he's kicking my butt with it," I said. "You want to hold him?"

"No, man." Ricky smiled. "I don't like holding white guys."

We were playing strong and together, and they were relying on two men, number 14 and Scott. Ruffy had taken Scott out of their offense, but he was still kicking it on defense and keeping the score close. The traffic at the top of the key was brutal. They were running me into picks like they had a schedule. If I had run into a school bus, I wouldn't have been surprised.

Ruffy was calling them from the center at first; then it got to be so many it was funny.

"Pick left! They're doubling! Slide! Go through!"

The game got down to thirty seconds and they had the ball. We were up by two and 14 was bringing the ball down again. I wanted to foul him, give him the two from the foul line right away, and then go for the win, but we didn't have any time-outs left so I couldn't do it. I knew 14 was happy to have the ball. He looked confident even though his team was a deuce down. I was hoping he would bring the ball in to Scott, because if he did, Ruffy was going to clobber the big man and put him on the foul line.

I stopped the ball five feet from the three-point line. The moment I stepped up, 14 turned his back to me, faked left, hooked me hard with his right elbow, and took a step around me.

It was like the whole thing was in slow motion. As I turned, I felt how low he was and how close and felt myself stopping so I wouldn't trip over him. As soon as I stopped, going up on the balls of my feet, I knew the rest of the program. He spun around me, and I turned to see his elbow go up past my eyes.

The only thing I could hope for was that he'd miss the trey. He didn't. They were up by a point.

Number 14 had pulled the same move on me twice, and I felt like crap as I glanced up at the clock. Eleven seconds.

Ricky brought the ball down quickly. I didn't want to look at the clock, but my eyes went up anyway. Six seconds. Not enough time to set anything up. Ricky made a move toward the basket, had a chance for a short jumper, then passed the ball out to me. Number 14 went for a head fake and I was past him. I took a quick step across the lane, saw Sky pick his forward, and went up as hard as I could.

All I saw was the big black shadow going up in the air between me and the hoop. I looked up to see if I could dunk, but I would have had to slam the ball through Scott's chest. His hands were a foot over the rim and the dude was still rising. I brought the ball back down and turned as I pulled it around my back, hoping that Tomas would be somewhere in the area.

I landed on my heels and fell hard on my back. As I bounced on one of the mats they had around the edge of the floor, I heard the buzzer. Time was out.

I looked up and saw our guys jumping up and down. Something good must have happened.

The guys helped me up and I looked at the scoreboard. Our score was flashing. We had won by a point.

"I was hoping you were sliding over!" I shouted to Tomas over the noise.

"I wasn't," Tomas said. "Their guy just pushed me away from him and the ball came to me!"

In the locker room we were all shouting and giving each other high fives. House was talking about how the backdoor play had worked at the end and how he was glad we remembered it.

The whole team felt good after the win, and it showed. We were slapping each other on the back and making stupid jokes and laughing even though they weren't that funny. House joined in, and so did Fletch.

"You know, we are a good team," Tomas said to me and Ruffy as we walked down the street. "I thought we could be—now I know it's true."

Ruffy laughed and said if it hadn't been for his nine points, we would have lost. Then he had to grab a cab and get home in a hurry. Me and Tomas kept talking as we walked, going over the game, enjoying ourselves.

Harlem is good when the temperature drops. The lazy rhythms of summer perk up and the street life seems to take on a sense of purpose. The cold-weather hustle is meaner, too. You can't be sleeping in the park with the hawk nipping at your butt, and the same Mr. Hungry who was kidding with you in July grows teeth when the weather turns cold.

Tomas said, "I'm going to make myself some soup and then I'm going to watch television, but the whole time I'm watching, I'm going to be thinking about the game."

"Why don't you come to my house for supper?" I said.

"Sure, why not?" Tomas nodded as he spoke. "What time should I come?"

"Six thirty," I said, trying to remember what time we usually had supper.

I hadn't thought about inviting Tomas to dinner, but I didn't think my mom would mind. Ruffy was always dropping by, and she always put out a plate for him.

When Tomas turned to go to his crib, I stopped him and asked if his mother was going to come by, too, just so I could let my mother know.

"No, she's working downtown tonight," he said.

I was thinking about the game when I reached the block. Some girls were jumping rope in front of the barbershop, and I watched while a fat chick did double Dutch. She was good.

I peeked into the barbershop to see who was there and saw Duke, who used to own the shop, and the other regulars.

"Drew, what's happening on the youth front these days?" Duke asked.

"Nothing much," I said. "Just came from playing ball."

"You win?" a tall, light-skinned guy asked.

"He said he just came from playing ball," Duke said. "If he had lost, he wouldn't be mentioning it."

"Yo, that's not true, sir," I said.

"You win?"

"Yeah, but . . ."

"The last time you lost—did you run in here and tell everybody?"

"You too hard, Duke."

I left the barbershop and went on upstairs.

The guys at the barbershop were right. I was happy because we had won. And just the way I could see where some people didn't think much about it, I knew I did think it was the bomb. No matter what House had said, ball made my heart beat faster, made me want to jump up and down and be Superman. That's what life was about anyway, being Superman and living like life itself was important. Basketball made my life important.

"Yo, Mom, I invited a friend to dinner tonight. He'll be here at six thirty."

"Who?" Jocelyn asked.

"*You did what?*" Mom asked.

"Tomas," I said. "The new guy I told you about on the team."

"The white boy?" Jocelyn asked.

Mom went into hyperdrive getting supper ready. She liked having people over, but she liked having time to get supper ready. Even Jocelyn lent a hand.

Mom made the pork tenderloin she had bought for Sunday and cooked that with green beans, carrots, mashed potatoes, and sauerkraut. Jocelyn was just heating up the gravy when Tomas knocked on the door.

Mom made a lot of noise about how tall Tomas was, and he smiled a lot and checked out the crib.

Our apartment was okay. Mom kept it spotless, and it usually looked good unless Jocelyn got a decorating idea and Mom let her mess with something. She let Jocelyn do just about anything she wanted to do, so sometimes we'd have pillows lying around that we weren't supposed to move, sit on, or put anything on.

"They're designer pillows," Jocelyn said.

When she first started putting her "designer" stuff around, I used to kid with her by sitting on them or throwing them at her, but she would always get even by taking the laces out of my shoes, which really pissed me off.

"So what kind of food did you eat in Prague?" Jocelyn asked Tomas when Mom had finished blessing the table.

"We had this same kind of food," Tomas said. "Pork with sauerkraut and knedliky."

"Sauerkraut and *what*?"

"Knedliky." Tomas repeated the word. "It's kind

of like dumplings in your country."

"So which is better, dumplings or ca-nade-li-key?" Jocelyn asked.

"Jocelyn, Tomas doesn't want to compare different kinds of food for you," Mom said.

"Yes, he does," Jocelyn said. "That's why he came over. Isn't that right, Tomas?"

"I think they're about the same," Tomas said.

"So why did you come to the United States, anyway?" Jocelyn asked.

"Jocelyn!" Mom's eyes grew wide.

"Well, in 2000 we had a big flood in Prague," Tomas said. "All the houses in my neighborhood were flooded. We didn't have a lot to begin with, but then we lost most of what we had left when the floods came. My father had died two years before, so my mother and I thought we would start all over again in a different place."

"I'm sorry to hear that, Tomas," Mom said.

"So tell me, Tomas." Jocelyn was on a roll. "What's it like being white?"

"Jocelyn, that's enough!" Mom was getting annoyed.

"You are a little sister," Tomas said, pointing a

finger at Jocelyn. "Nothing is worse than a little sister. In Prague if you have a little sister, you don't have to pay taxes, because having a little sister is bad enough."

"Jocelyn, Tomas is our guest," Mom said.

"All I need to know now, Mama, is does he have a girlfriend?" Jocelyn said.

"I have seven girlfriends," Tomas said. "One for each day of the week."

"Which means you don't have any girlfriend, because if you had one, you'd be bragging about it." Jocelyn was pleased with herself. "Drew almost had a girlfriend, but then she came to her senses. What's your favorite subject in school?"

"I thought all you wanted to know was if he had a girlfriend," Mom said.

"And she doesn't care what your favorite subject is if it's not math," I said.

"It's not math," Tomas said.

"Then I guess I'll just have to keep looking," Jocelyn said.

I didn't know why Jocelyn liked Tomas, but she did. He was easy to get along with and pleased Mom when he asked for more food. After dinner we hung in my room for a while, and he looked over my CDs.

"The coach told me he thought we could make it all the way to the state championship if we played together as a team," he said.

"We have five more games before we reach the regionals," I said. "Only one team makes the regionals from each division. If we win the regionals, we play in the state finals. We've already lost one game. We lose two and we could be gone. Bryant hasn't lost yet."

"You think this is a good team?" Tomas asked.

"Yeah. What do you think?"

"It's a good team," he said. "Faster than my team in Prague."

What I was thinking was that he wasn't sure. He knew what the guys on his team in Prague were like, but he didn't know what a black team from Harlem was all about. He said that our team was faster than the team in Europe, but I wondered what other things he had seen that were different. I also wondered what House had said to him.

hen Tomas left, Mom got on Jocelyn, but I could tell she wasn't serious. Both of them had liked him. I was surprised at Jocelyn, because she doesn't take to people that quickly. I looked over my homework assignments, did some of the reading in history, and started to do the math. But I must have fallen asleep, because the next thing I knew, Mom was waking me up, asking me if I was going to have breakfast. "And why you sleeping in your clothes?" she asked.

"In case I had to go somewhere in my dreams," I said.

"You know, you and your sister don't act like anybody in my family," Mom said, standing in the doorway. "My side of the family thinks slower and talks slower, too. You're both fast thinkers, but you're not slick or nothing. I like that."

I wasn't fast enough to figure out what that meant, so I let it go.

After school Ruffy called me and asked if I wanted to go downtown with him and Tony. I was surprised that Tony was back on the street.

"They set a trial date for three months from now," Ruffy said. "And Tony's out on bail."

I felt good about that and said I would go downtown with them. We met in front of the bank on 145th and Tony flagged down a cab. We went down to the Old Navy store on 125th Street, and Tony bought some dynamite shirts. Then we walked down to the African restaurant on Lenox Ave. Tony said we should order what we wanted.

"I got you covered," he said, flashing some twenties.

I wondered where he got the money, but I didn't say anything. Ruffy was talking about how Mr. Brunson,

Tony's lawyer, wanted Tony to dress for the trial.

"He wants him clean, but not too flashy," he said. "Kind of conservative, like me."

"It's all a game, man," Tony said. "What I got to figure out is if I really want to deal with a trial or not."

"What are the other two guys going to do?" I asked.

"Depends on me," Tony said. He was leaning back in his chair. "If I take the deal they want to hand down, I can burn both of them. You know what I mean? What they got is a whole bunch of things—my lawyer calls it a laundry list—we're being charged with. There's three ways this deal can go. I can cop the deal and do a three-to-five bid, and probably get back into the world in twenty-nine months. Or I can take my chance on the trial and maybe walk away clean. But if they throw a curve and I get a guilty verdict, then I'm facing a whole stack of calendars. So I got to check it all out and weigh the pros and cons and make my decision."

Tony was acting like he was making a real-estate deal or something instead of talking about going to jail.

"Brunson wants him to take the deal," Ruffy said.

"You know, that's all good for him," Tony came back. "He can say he won something because I got a light bid. But I ain't buying no time just to make him look good. You know what I mean?"

"Yeah," I said.

Tony kept on talking about his big decision and how he had figured out his chances for this and that, as if he were in control of everything. It sounded foul to me.

"Norman and Little G got records, so they're facing heavy time all around," Tony said. "They scared of me copping, because if I cop, I can send them away forever."

Yeah, right. I was glad when we finished eating and left the restaurant. Tony said he was going to grab a cab and go over to the projects to see his girlfriend. Ruffy was supposed to go with him and then take the cab home. I said I was going to drop by the Studio Museum to pick up a book for Jocelyn and would see Ruffy in the morning.

Tony and Ruffy got into a cab and headed east. I watched them go for a bit and then started walking uptown.

Tony's attitude had bothered me a lot. He was spending money I knew he must have got from his mother and talking about his decision to take the plea deal as if he were on top of things, when he was really just running his mouth about how much time he was going to be locked up.

Me and Ruffy were sitting in the restaurant with him, and both of us knew what the deal was. But we hadn't spoken on it because there really wasn't that much to say. The time when Tony could have made a good decision was gone. Now all he could pull together was the least pain. He was acting tough because that's all he could pull off, but it wasn't even his game anymore. It was the prosecutor's game and the judge's game. They had all the rules and all the moves, and all Tony had was his front, and that was raggedy.

It was turning colder, and a few snow flurries were coming down along Frederick Douglass Boulevard. I tried to remember the last time there had been a heavy snow in Harlem. It had to have been at least a year or so. The cold wasn't that bad, and the walk uptown felt good. My head was clear and I wanted to push my mind on what I had to get done for school, but I kept thinking about Tony and how he had let his life slip away. I wondered if there was a time, just one second, that he could have made one move, one step to the right or left, or said one word different and found himself in a whole other place. I wondered, if I got to that moment, whether I would see it clear. I felt sad for Tony, but I felt nervous for me, too.

The next game was with Wheatley. Wheatley wasn't a good team. All they could do was run up and down the court and heave the ball. They had five lames on their starting team and ten more lames on the bench.

"You know how these guys play?" Ernie asked. "They play like black popcorn, man. They're just popping around the court and running all over the place and hoping that the ball comes to them. They don't have any talent."

We started off great and jumped to a 15–6 lead. We hung on to those nine points for the first half with House congratulating us because nobody was in foul trouble. I passed as much as I could, trying to get everybody into the game. At halftime their cheerleaders came out. The trip was that their boosters were all fat. Ernie and Sky were cracking on them when two big greasy dudes came out of the stands and said they were going to pop a cap in Sky someplace nice so he wouldn't have to worry about using Preparation H anymore. Ernie started mouthing off to the guy, but I cooled him down.

"Look around you, Ernie," I said, leaning over him. "We're in their gym, in their school, and there's a hundred and fifty ugly-butt guys up there who haven't got anything better to do tonight than stomp us to death!"

"I'll let you slide this time, fool!" Ernie said to the guy, who looked like Busta Rhymes on a bad hair day.

"Man, shut up before we pull a drive-by on y'alls bench!" the guy said.

I believed him. Anyway, we went out and finished strong to win by fourteen points. In my mind the win wasn't good because Wheatley didn't have much of a team.

House heard something was going to go down, so we didn't shower, just grabbed our clothes and jumped on the bus. The driver, seeing we were

getting on his bus funky, didn't waste any time getting out of there, either.

We had four games to go and we were coming together real strong. House had us practicing hard whenever we weren't playing. He had Ruffy in the weight room, and my man was looking good. He wasn't really cut, but he was beefy and had lost enough weight to get down the court faster. He had always been strong inside, with his boxing out making up for his not being able to really sky too tough.

We had killed Tech before. Everybody killed Tech, because they didn't have no team. What they did have was Cleo Hill.

"If that boy had a coach, he could be all-world," Fletch said. "He's got the size, the heart, and a few moves, but his coach won't let him do what he does best, hang under the boards."

What they had Cleo doing was trying to score from all over the court. He had a little outside jumper that was nice, like Brandon Walters, who played down on West 4th Street. What he didn't have was a consistent touch around the hoop. Sometimes, when you got him real mad, he would just go crazy and score a bunch of points in a hurry. The games they won went that way. It was close down to the end, and then somebody got Cleo mad.

We played Tech and ate them up. No contest. Cleo brought the ball down the court near the end of the game and went around Tomas with a crossover dribble. I anticipated the whole thing and went up and knocked his shot away and everybody goofed on that. Then, when I had the ball, I came down, put a move on Cleo that left him standing in his tracks, and went up for the slam. Cleo recovered, came back, and got my stuff from the back. I tried to force the ball through the hoop, but he just pulled me down to the floor with one huge hand.

"How you like that, pretty boy?" he said.

After the game Sky got on my case, asking me why I changed my mind when I went for the slam.

"That must be a new kind of move, man," he said. "Bring the ball up, get a mean look on your face, and then come down to the floor and grin!"

"Anytime you're up against some real players, somebody is going to throw your stuff away," I said. "He just got mine."

. . .

Wednesday practice. Of all the practice sessions we went through, the one everybody hated most is the OK Corral drill. Everybody except Fletch. He was the one who dreamed the sucker up, and we had to hear his lecture every time we ran it.

"Every game you play, there are six times when you're supposed to get an easy basket under the bucket and somebody throws it away," he said. "If you throw the ball too soft, you let everybody make a grab for it. If you throw it too hard, you're going to throw it out-of-bounds or somebody is going to miss it so's it goes out-of-bounds. You have to learn to catch the ball and throw it short distances to recover those six easy shots."

We stood in threes in the paint a few feet from the boards, six feet apart, making two passes as fast as we could before going for the layup without putting the ball on the floor. I was with Needham and Tomas. Needham couldn't catch a cool breeze in an igloo, but Tomas had good hands. We worked on short passes for twenty minutes before House let us go.

Most of the team started toward the shower,

but I saw House stop Tomas and Abdul and point them back onto the court. Fletch was waiting with a basketball under the basket. I sat down to see what they were going to do.

What was happening was that Fletch was working with Tomas. He was using Abdul as the defensive player. I watched as he pulled out the tape and made an X on the floor with it. Position play. For the next twenty minutes Fletch worked with Tomas, passing the ball in to him from the top of the key or from the sideline to either side of the X, making him move to the X in one dribble and then go for the shot.

He did it over and over, with Fletch yelling at him, telling him when he was doing it wrong, telling him when his feet were too slow or he was bringing the ball too low.

"Make them stop your strongest move!"

I watched as Tomas moved his wide body through the lane, pivoting on the tape and going for the basket. Tomas did it over and over again. Pulling the ball closer to his chest when Fletch told him to chin it, extending his arms when Fletch told him to get bigger, shaking his head when Fletch asked him if he was getting tired.

129

I felt sick. I felt angry. Not just anger, but a rage coming up in me. I wanted to stand up and walk away, but as tight as my arms felt, as huge as my chest felt, my legs were weak.

I thought Fletch was supposed to be on my side. Why was he talking to me softly and then building up Tomas?

I looked around, sure that I would find House gloating somewhere, leaning against the tiled walls, but he wasn't anywhere in the gym. It was just Tomas and Abdul and Fletch, and me standing on the side feeling my guts ache.

As they walked off the court, I saw that Abdul was dripping in sweat. Tomas's legs, heavy and white and hairy, moved like tree stumps toward the locker room. Fletch stopped a few feet from me. I looked up at him. I didn't have enough saliva in my mouth to spit.

"How you feeling, Drew?" he asked.

"I see you're working with the white boy," I said.

"What do you want, Drew?" Fletch looked at me. "You want to get over by having him fall down? That what you want?"

"Get out my face!" I said.

Fletch stepped closer to me. "What you going to do, Drew? You going to hit me? Is that what you want to do?" he asked. "Because if you want to give up your game altogether, that's the way to do it. Raise your hands and see how far your anger gets you."

We glared at each other for a long time; then he pivoted on one foot and walked away

Game day. When Powell came to our gym, I was feeling down. What I wished was that I could jump up and hit somebody, just do a real beat down on the world and get it out of my system. I knew what Fletch had said was real, but I was feeling so frustrated, I didn't know what to do with myself. Maybe for the first time in my life I didn't want to play ball.

Powell had Donald Hand and this tough-shooting Italian guy, Frankie Corsetto. If Donald brought his mind to the game, he'd be real good. What he does bring his mind to is being a thug. The word on the street is that he took money from shorties and did some boosting down on 1-2-5. You can stop Frankie if you foul him a lot because he doesn't like to get hit and will throw up only treys if you bang him.

I felt sluggish, and everything I did was wrong. The first time I got the ball, I traveled. The next time I got it, I threw up an air ball. Meanwhile, Frankie is going around me and I'm trying to hit him but he's making me look bad and House sits me.

At the end of the first quarter they're up by six, but we come back, with me sitting on the bench, and at the half it's all tied. I was mad and feeling bad at the same time. It was like my whole life was going down the drain.

We came out with four minutes left in the intermission and ran a few layups before the start of the second half. The whole team was down, and Sky's Hollywood pep talk wasn't doing anything to help. By the end of the third quarter we were losing by seven. I had started the second half, but House had me on the bench again.

I watched Tomas play. He and Ruffy were both working deep, changing the game, making Powell play in unfamiliar territory. I thought about the X that Fletch had made on the floor. For the first time Tomas was leading the scoring.

We got into the last quarter, and Sky fouled out

with four minutes to play and us behind by five. House looked at the bench and called Needham's number.

"No, man!" Ernie got into House's face. "Bring Drew in! I don't want to lose this game!"

"Don't tell me how to run this team!" House pushed Ernie away.

Fletch stepped between House and Ernie and whispered something in House's ear.

Whatever Fletch said pissed House off, because he gave him the hardest look I had ever seen.

House didn't say anything. He pointed to me and made a thumbing motion to the floor.

Fletch came over to me. "Don't disappoint yourself, Drew," he said.

I checked the time. Four minutes and two seconds. I knew I had to bust it big-time.

One of their men was on the foul line for a one-and-one. He made both shots, which put them up seven. I brought the ball down with Ernie and watched Ruffy come out for the high pick. He wanted me to go around Frankie. I faked left and ducked in toward the pick. Somehow Frankie got past Ruffy and was on my case when I hit the paint.

Their center was already sliding over when I went up. Their big man wasn't that good, but he got all ball and slapped my shot away. The ref blew the whistle and signaled foul.

Their coach jumped up but it didn't do any good. I still got the shots and made them both. Back down to five.

They tried slowing the game, but we pressed them and got a close-guarding call and possession. Ernie threw up a three that banged off the rim, and Ruffy got the bound and threw it to Tomas. Tomas looked around and threw the ball out, almost giving it back, and we set up again.

This time Ernie cut across the middle, passed to Tomas, who handed it off to Ruffy, who made the layup.

They made a deuce on a short jumper and we cut it to three again on a long pass to Ernie from Ruffy when the guy guarding him fell asleep or something.

With a minute and five seconds left, Frankie brought the ball down again and passed it to Donald. Donald cut across the top of the key and got past Ernie, but Ruffy cracked him in his ribs with a righteous elbow. He doubled up for a moment and then told Ruffy what he was going to do to him after the game. That was a joke, because nobody messed with Ruffy without a piece.

Donald missed the first half of the one-and-one and I copped the bound. We flew downcourt and I found myself one-on-one with Donald. I gave him a head fake to the left, then went to the left and almost by him when he hit me. The ball rolled off my fingertips, against the backboard, rolled on the rim, and fell through.

I was standing on the foul line when I realized that the ref hadn't called a foul.

We were still trailing by one and they had the ball. Frankie held one finger up. I glanced at the clock and saw there was too much time to hold the ball for one shot, so I figured it must be a play. They were spreading the floor, and we were playing tight around the key. I motioned for the guys to go out after the ball. We didn't want to give them a last shot if they were up, and we didn't want to give up a late three, either.

Ernie went after Frankie big-time, slapping at the ball with one hand while putting his hand on

Frankie's butt with the other. That messes with a lot of guys, but Frankie didn't give up the ball, so I left my man and double-teamed him.

Frankie passed the ball behind his back, through me and Ernie, to their center. Donald had slipped around me and could have cut for the deuce, but instead of that he tried to mess with Ruffy, I guess because Ruffy had fouled him before. I caught up with Donald just as their center threw up a sky hook from the foul line. I blocked Donald out and he went over my back, but the ball still came to me.

I passed it out to Ernie and we were heading downcourt. Ruffy got the ball at the foul line, faked a move, and spotted Abdul picking off Tomas's man. Ruffy passed the ball in, and Donald went toward the board. What happened was that Donald didn't think he could stop the shot but he was blocking out for the board. The only thing was that Tomas didn't shoot the ball.

"Shoot!" Ernie shouted.

Tomas froze, looking around. I got to him and snatched the ball from his hand and went up, releasing the ball just as the buzzer sounded. The game was over. I turned as I came down and saw the referee signaling that the basket counted. We had won.

The Chargers were heading off the floor, fists pumping, when I felt something grab my arm. I was off-balance as I was spun around.

"What did you do that for!" It was Tomas.

I had never seen Tomas mad before, but I didn't care if he was mad or not. I was being cool when I turned away again, and he was being very uncool when he spun me around again.

"I asked you a question!" he yelled into my face. "When I ask you a question, you answer me!"

"Later for you, fool!"

Tomas started toward me again, and Ruffy grabbed him around the waist, lifted him off the ground, and slammed him to the gym floor. He started to get up and Abdul pushed him down again and told him to chill before he got killed.

By this time Fletch and Mr. Barker, who had been at the game, had rushed over and were pushing us toward the locker room.

"C'mon, guys! C'mon!" Mr. Barker was big and strong. "Everybody cool down."

I didn't know what was bugging Tomas. We had

won. House came over and knelt next to him on the floor. He looked all right to me, and I started toward the locker room.

"What's his problem?" Ruffy asked.

I shrugged. Tomas seemed to be tripping, but I didn't know why.

In the shower it was the old team, joking around and talking through the game. Sky found out he had five assists and was making sure that everybody knew that.

"That's how Telfair got to the NBA," he said. "He made all those assists in the All-Star Game. You remember that from the DVD?"

House had made sure everybody on the team had the DVD and knew how a street dude from Brooklyn had made it to the NBA by hard work.

Tomas didn't shower; neither did Colin. They were waiting in House's office while the team got dressed. House called me and Ruffy in and told us to sit down. Mr. Barker was there too, leaning against the wall, looking good in his gray silk suit and yellow tie.

"I'm thinking of suspending both of you for the last games," House said. "I think you're trying to start racial discord on this team."

"Yeah, I am," I said. "That's why I ran up behind him and spun him around and yelled in his face. Or was that him putting his hands on me?"

"Why did you take the ball from me?" Tomas said.

"Because I don't like guys from Prague," I said.

"And I don't like guys from Africa," Tomas came back. "You think you got all the moves and you're the only one who can play basketball. But your moves don't make you the man. I can play as well as you can. I see you and I'm not impressed."

"Yeah, and you're all-world, huh?"

"I think everybody should apologize to everybody else and start enjoying the win," Mr. Barker said. "So why don't you guys just shake hands and move on?"

"I don't tolerate fighting on my team," House said. "I haven't decided what I'm going to do about this, and I'm the one running this team."

"*We* haven't decided yet," Mr. Barker said, putting the emphasis on *we*. "And I'm the one running this school. Right now we're all going home, or at least we're going to leave the building."

House wasn't happy with that, but we all left.

It was cold as me and Ruffy made our way down into the valley. I thanked him for getting my back.

"I needed to slam somebody anyway," he said. "Something to talk about instead of Tony."

"How's he doing?" I asked.

A skinny dude with crack-shiny eyes stopped us, let us glimpse a watch, and shoved it back into his pocket. "You need a Rolex?" he asked, looking around. "Fifty dollars."

"Where am I going to get fifty dollars?" Ruffy asked.

"Ten dollars because you look like a right-on brother," Shiny Eyes said.

"I ain't got it, my man." Ruffy held his hands up as we walked by.

"Poor-ass punks!"

"So what you think about Tomas?" I asked as we crossed the street.

"He might have to get his butt kicked to realize this is our hood and not his," Ruffy said. "When people get stuff handed to them too easy, they think they deserved it."

I hadn't thought of it that way. Tomas probably figured he was just supposed to get to Baldwin and take over the team.

I got home and Jocelyn was standing on a chair in the kitchen running her mouth. Mom signaled for me to sit down. I didn't want to, but I did want to hear what Jocelyn was up on the chair for.

" . . . So, my loyal subjects, I have had to make a difficult and painful decision. Now many of you might wonder why a perfect person like me has to make hard decisions. . . ."

"Jocelyn, say what you have to say, please," Mom said.

"I have passed the test for Stuyvesant High School and now must decide if I am to remain at Baldwin—"

I put my hands out and Jocelyn slapped me five. Stuyvesant was big-time to math and science nuts, and Jocelyn had wanted to go there ever since she was in the fifth grade, so I knew what "painful" answer she was going to come up with.

Mom listened to the whole speech, smiling and nodding her head just the way Jocelyn knew she would. Later, when Jocelyn came banging on my door—like I knew she would—I asked her to spare me the dramatics.

Jocelyn said, "As I was saying to Mae Jamison the other day—you know me and her are like this?"

"You and the first black woman astronaut? I should have known it."

"Yeah, anyway, I was telling Mae that I was ready to take my place in the space program. And I'm starting at Stuyvesant."

"Why don't you launch yourself from your room?" I asked.

She gave me a wink as she left. The girl was okay.

It was almost ten o'clock when Mom opened the door and told me that there was a phone call for me.

"It's that boy who came here that day," she said.

When I got to the phone, I heard Tomas and somebody, probably his mother, talking in some foreign language. I listened for a while but I couldn't understand anything, so I said hello.

"Hello, this is Tomas Dvorski," he said.

"Tell him you're sorry," I heard his mother say in the background.

"Why you take the ball from me?" he asked.

"Time was running out," I said. "Why didn't you shoot the ball?"

"I was waiting for the last second," Tomas said. "Then you took the ball."

"Hey, we won," I said.

"You don't do that again or I won't play with you," he said.

"Say you're sorry!" came again in the background.

"Don't play," I said. "I don't care." Then I hung up.

"What was that all about?" Mom asked.

"Nothing," I said.

Tomas had me pissed. Anytime anybody gets really mad at me, it makes me really mad at them, too. In a way I could dig where he was coming from, because I did take the ball from him. But I didn't think he was waiting for the last minute. His inside game wasn't all that hot, so his shot wasn't going to be a sure thing and he had to know it. The dude just froze. Still, he wanted the chance and I knew where that was coming from. He was talking from his gut, and I was down with that.

Lying across my bed, I was thinking about Tomas's mother telling him to apologize. He was mad at me because he thought I was dissing his game, and I was mad at House because I thought he was dissing my game. Something had gone down between Fletch and House during the game, and they were dealing with each other. It was like everybody had their own thing going and it all mattered big-time but it was all different.

If Tomas had taken the ball from me, I might have punched his lights out. Maybe I shouldn't have taken the ball. But then, maybe, we wouldn't have copped the W.

The next day in school there was some back-and-forth about how Ruffy had put Tomas on the ground, but I stayed away from it. I was trying to be cool. Like my man Othello, I was trying to be bigger than the small stuff.

The second period ended and I was going toward the media center when I saw Tomas in the hallway. He stopped and glared at me as I came near him. I guessed that was supposed to mean something. I stopped a few feet from him and glared back.

"I'm getting tired of you," he said.

"If you got something you need to say with your hands," I said, "speak up or get out my face."

I think he was measuring me, wondering if he could take me. I had an answer for him if he had the nerve to put the question out there. Hell, no.

He walked away, but he was ready. He wasn't backing down, just not dishing in school.

Practice. House was cutting daggers at me like he wanted to do me some serious harm. We didn't have any drills, just worked on getting the ball inbounds and ran a few plays off the high pick with Ruffy and Abdul taking turns at center. I wondered if House was going to start Abdul. Abdul was okay, but he wasn't big enough to play center, and he wasn't as good as Ruffy anyway.

Fletch came over to me at the end of practice. When House saw him start to talk to me, he called him. Fletch said he'd see him in a minute.

"Now!" House shot back.

Fletch turned his back to House and put his arm around me. "Don't let what's happening off the court get on the court and mess with your game," he said.

"Whatever."

"And I said the same thing to Tomas," he said. Then he walked away.

Boys & Girls had DeShaun Williams. He was six-nine and skinny. He claimed he was only eighteen, but he had three kids and one of them was going to school already. Jocelyn and her girl friend Ramona came to the game, and I pointed him out to her and asked her if she thought he was only eighteen.

"Probably," Jocelyn said. "I know his whole family. They're all ugly. That's how ugly looks when it's stretched out like that."

Boys & Girls should have been a good team, but they laid everything on DeShaun. Their team stood around and waited for him to throw them the ball. Ruffy's job was just to keep him off the boards, and it wasn't easy because he was strong and he kept swinging his elbows. On defense I helped to block out as much as I could or else went over and helped bang on DeShaun.

On offense they were letting us go by, but DeShaun was knocking everything away. The first quarter ended with a sloppy 13–13 score and we had a bunch of turnovers. We were up at the half 37–27.

The whole second half was stupid ball, with Boys & Girls turning the ball over like they didn't want to win. I made sure that I fed Tomas inside a few times, and he made sure that he blocked out when I took my man to the hoop. It was like we were showing respect but without the feeling.

We half won the game and they half lost it. We were changing and Tomas came over and hit me on the leg.

"Nice game," he said.

"Your mama tell you to say that?" I asked him.

"Yeah," he said, smiling.

I got home, and my mother's sister, Aunt Ethel, was there with her husband's father, Mr. Cephus.

The old fellow fascinated me because he was nearly blind but he was always sharp. Aunt Ethel said he dressed himself. Plus he had become rich working as a mechanic or rebuilding cars, something like that. He was kind of a typical old dude because he always asked how we were and then started talking about himself before you had a chance to answer.

"So what's going on in your life, young Mr. Drew?" he asked me.

"Not much," I said. "Just going to school, playing a little ball—you know, same old thing."

"Well, that's good," he said. "You know, I used to play baseball back when they had Negro Leagues."

"I've heard a lot about the Negro League," I said.

"Not Negro League," he said, turning his head away from me. "Negro Leagues. There was more than one Negro league. There were the big-time leagues that everybody knows about because white writers talk about them, and then there were the little leagues around the country. There was a Kansas City Monarchs out in Kansas City and there was the Monarchs right here in New York. That's who I played for."

"It must have been frustrating knowing you could

play ball as good as the white players and not be able to get into the Major Leagues." Jocelyn had come in and sat in the armchair across from Mr. Cephus.

"Not for me it wasn't," Mr. Cephus said. He moved his head away again, and I knew that little move must have just been about something he felt inside.

"It would have been for me," Jocelyn said.

"It wasn't for me because I couldn't play no ball!" Mr. Cephus said. "I could field a little, but everybody knew I couldn't hit a fastball to save my soul. Did I tell you I once batted against Bob Feller, the white guy who went into the Hall of Fame?"

"No, you didn't," I answered.

"Well, I wasn't blind then," Mr. Cephus went on. "But I might have been, because that young boy was throwing smoke across that plate and all I saw was a blur out on the mound, followed by a large pop when that ball hit the catcher's glove. Man, he could pitch."

"But you still played?" Jocelyn asked.

"Yeah, I played. I had a dream that I wanted to be something special. I thought it was baseball until I played it. I played for two years and I knew it wasn't going to be about baseball."

"Then you went into cars?" I asked.

"No, I always worked around cars," Mr. Cephus said. "After I left baseball—or baseball left me—I got into the antique business. Read a lot of books about it and learned to prance around like I knew something."

"That's a good business," Jocelyn said.

Mom looked in, saw me and Jocelyn talking with Mr. Cephus, and gave us a Mom smile before ducking back into the kitchen to talk with Aunt Ethel.

"That wasn't no good business for a black man, because black people don't want old furniture and they don't care if you call it an antique or not," Mr. Cephus said. "Then when they get to the point they do want antiques, they're so white they need to go buy it from the white dealers. You see what I mean?"

"Yeah, I do," I said.

"People told me to give up trying to be special and settle down to a regular life. There ain't nothing wrong with a regular life, and that's the Lord's truth," Mr. Cephus said. "But it wasn't for me, because I wanted to be something special. I didn't care what it was going to be or how it was going to be special, but I wanted to be special. I thought I might have to go out and rob a bank or something. So when people started pointing their fingers at me and smiling up their sleeves, it didn't bother me none. I believed in my little dream even though it wasn't doing exactly what I wanted it to do.

"Sometimes I felt like I was coming home to my dream—walking in the front door—and Mr. Reality was sneaking out the back door with a grin on his face. I knew how easy it was for a dream to die. I seen that all around me. You could let it die by just looking the other way—you know, some of those Asian people say they don't kill nothing, but they'll take a fish out of water and lay it on the ground and then say it just died on its own—you can do that with a dream, too. And sometimes you can get so frustrated, you feel so bad about your dream, that you go on and kill it yourself. When you do that, you're killing a piece of yourself, too."

"So did you get to be special?" Jocelyn asked.

"Yeah, I did, girl." Mr. Cephus smiled as he shook his head. "I was working in a car repair business, and every once in a while I got my hands on a car that I could fix up and resell. That worked out pretty good, and after a while I bought a couple of houses and fixed them up and resold them. Before I knew it, I had made enough money for people in Harlem to start calling me mister. When I made enough money for the white folks downtown to start calling me mister—then guess what?"

"You knew you were special," Jocelyn said.

"Do tell!" Mr. Cephus slapped his knee and started laughing out loud. Mama and Aunt Ethel came in to see what was going on, and Mr. Cephus started telling the same story all over again, beginning with the Negro Leagues.

The news about Bryant reached the neighborhood about a quarter past six. Three guys and a girl called to give it to me. Boogie had been thrown out on a technical late in the last quarter, and Bryant had lost to Warrick. We had a chance to win the division and move to the next level. All we had to do was beat Bryant with Boogie in the game.

The story was in the hood that night and all around the city in the morning. Kids in school who didn't know squat about ball were running around talking about the big game coming up. The teacher's aide who made the announcements in the morning wished the team luck and said that she hoped we got more runs than Bryant. Right.

Sporting News sent a photographer and a reporter to our practice. The reporter said that he had talked to the Bryant coach, and he was glad that it was a showdown between the two best teams.

House said us against Bryant was like the old rivalries between Lincoln and Grady in the B League.

The photographer took a lot of pictures, mostly of Tomas and way too many of Colin. They even took a picture of Colin standing on a chair up near the rim as if he were dunking.

"If he wanted to slam during a game, I'd have to follow him around the floor with that chair," Sky said.

Soon as the guys from the paper left, House got down to business. We practiced some backdoors and everybody had to shoot fifty shots from the foul line.

"We can win or lose the game from the foul line," Fletch was saying. "You get tired, you get nervous, and you forget to bend your knees. Your body puts the ball in motion, not just your arms. If your body puts the ball in motion, you're going to make seventy-five percent of your shots. And don't do what Abdul likes to do, bend your knees, then straighten up before you take the shot. One smooth motion. Bryant lost by five points and they missed eight free throws. You can do the math. Anybody who can't figure that out, see me after practice!"

I did my free throws and hit thirty-one out of fifty. House asked me what my problem was and I said, "Nothing." That was a stupid question.

I sat down and watched Tomas go to the line. He hit forty-two out of fifty. Colin hit forty-two out of fifty, too.

"That's what white people do when they're not out in the street or going to work," Ernie said. "They shoot foul shots."

That was funny. I was just hoping they shot them that well against Bryant.

Back in the hood the weather was freaky warm and the garbage was stinking up the place. People had their windows closed, and someone even called the fire department to see what the smell was. It was just the garbage and the dirty street and the smell coming off the river.

We were going to play Bryant at our gym on Friday, and Mr. Barker called a special pep rally assembly on Wednesday morning. We all had to show up in our uniforms. The band played, and we were introduced one by one. It was definitely mad. Everybody was making noise, and Mr. Barker and House made speeches about how proud they were of the team and whatnot. A girl from the eleventh grade said that she was going to go out with the guy who made the most points. Abdul said he hoped it was him.

"Yo, Abdul, she's a skank!" Needham said when we reached the locker room. "She's liable to have congenital pregnancy or something!"

"Yo, check this out." Ernie called us in close. "Abdul finally found out that him and his sister are built different. Now he wants to know what that means."

"Don't talk about my sister," Abdul said.

"The only way that Abdul and his sister are built different is that her mustache is bigger than his," Sky chimed in.

Abdul got mad and pushed Sky, and we almost had a fight right there, but House and Ruffy broke it up.

"Save your fight for the game, guys," House said.

All day Friday I was nervous, thinking about the game. In English, Miss Tomita got on my case because my mind wasn't on the class discussion. She had wanted it to be on contrasting the character of Iago with the character of Roderigo, but it broke down into a fight between the girls and the boys. The boys thought that Othello should have killed Iago for lying on his woman.

"Or at least for putting his business in the street," one dude said.

The girls said that Iago and Othello were doing a man kind of thing and it was the chick who got iced.

I knew it was wrong to take Othello's side, but I could see where the brother was coming from. If the only thing he had going on was his rep and his woman, and all of a sudden it looked like she was running off and kicking his rep in the dust along the way, he would have to feel like he wanted to go to 187. It was wrong, but in a way I could still see it.

"So what you're saying, Mr. Lawson"—Miss Tomita had a hand on her little bony hip—"is that you would throw away your whole life because of what you *thought* was going on?"

"Yo, Miss T, can I think about it?"

"Think, my lord."

We met at the gym. House talked about getting everybody into the game and going after loose balls. We were telling some jokes, and I could see that all the guys were on edge as much as I was. And we all knew we weren't playing any chumps.

Game time. The Bryant team came by bus, but their student body came by train or bus or car. There must have been five hundred kids with Bryant's colors, maroon and gold. When our people saw that, they started coming in, too. Soon the whole gym was packed and cell phones were ringing everywhere. Baldwin's blue and white was at the west end of the court and Bryant's supporters were on the far end, away from the door.

"You see Boogie?" Ruffy asked me.

I looked over to where Bryant was running layups, and Boogie wasn't there. "You think he's going to play?"

"I don't know," Ruffy said. "I asked one of their guys about their last game, and he said some little white boy—number 14—got happy and threw in about two hundred threes. It wasn't just a technical."

"Why did Boogie get thrown out of the game?"

"There was a scramble on the floor and a guy bit him," Ruffy said, smiling. "Boogie punched him in the mouth and got thrown out."

I was glad to see that Ruffy was smiling.

The warning buzzer sounded, and all of a sudden we heard this big oooooooo! sound come from the Bryant side of the stands. We looked up, and they were bringing out signs and holding them up. I knew we shouldn't have looked, but we all did. The signs read BEWARE THE BOOGIE MAN! And then, from out of the crowd, in his warm-up suit, came James "Boogie" Simpson.

"Hey, Drew, you looking good." Boogie came over and put his arm around my shoulder. "You look like you eating Wheaties and lifting weights."

"No, you're the one eating Wheaties," I said. "I see you brought your fan club with you."

"Yeah, they came to see the Boogie Man." Boogie grinned.

He patted me on the shoulder and went back to his team's bench.

House got us together, and we stacked hands.

"Keep your heads in the game and play together," he said. "We need to stop the ball early so they don't set up their plays. This is our court and, if we want it bad enough, our game. On three—"

"One! Two! Three!" We broke and the game was on.

They copped the tap, and their two guard brought the ball down. We stopped the ball high and they forced it inside to their center, then threw it outside to Boogie. Boogie started his dribble outside the three-point line, and I came out to get him. I saw their big man come out to set a high pick. Boogie pointed to a spot on the floor and made a move toward him. I slid right and straightened up slightly to slide past him. Boogie made a quick move, I reached with my elbow to make contact on the pick, and Boogie made a crossover move to my left, which caught me leaning the wrong way.

Boogie's first step was outside my foot and his next step was down the lane with me trailing him. Tomas came over and went up with Boogie. No contest. Boogie slammed over Tomas and the Bryant crowd went wild. They were up by two.

Ernie brought the ball down for us and Boogie was on me tight. I went inside and cut across the baseline and then out looking for their forwards. I found one, leaned into him hard for a moment, then shot out toward the three-point line. The forward took a step after me, stopped, and turned toward his own man, but it was too late. Sky had slipped deep, taken Ernie's pass, and made the deuce.

I was tight. I kept my hands on Boogie when he didn't have the ball, and pushed him whenever he tried to go by me. Boogie was strong, but mostly he relied on his speed, and I wanted to make him use his strength. Our guys were more active than Bryant's, and if any of them tried to muscle his way to the hoop, we could double-team him and force the ball out.

We exchanged baskets again and everyone was feeling that the game was going well. The sneakers were squeaking on the newly polished floor as guys made good cuts. Bryant was trying to run plays, trying to establish an inside game against Ruffy, Tomas, and Sky, but it wasn't working, so the guards were controlling the ball more and more. Boogie was probing, looking for something weak he could work on. The crowd was calling his name, for him to do something spectacular, but he was concentrating on setting up patterns. He had his game face on, and I knew he was showing us respect, but he was digging for the win.

Their center could sky, but he had bad hands. He was getting to the bounds but he wasn't pulling them down cleanly. Plus whenever he had the ball, he would bring it down low and away from his body. Ernie tied him up twice and Sky stole the ball from him twice.

Boogie kept going to his left and I kept pushing him. Once he put a move on me and turned me around but drove into Tomas, and they called a charging foul on him. He grinned.

At the end of the first quarter it was Baldwin 18 and Bryant 15. Boogie had six points, and I had four. It was only a three-point lead, but I was feeling all right.

"You're playing good," House said to the team. "Keep the pressure on. You're switching well. Keep the pressure on."

Bryant decided to up the pressure, too, and came out with a full-court press. We didn't dig the press soon enough, and when Boogie stopped me, Ernie wasn't looking and everybody else was downcourt. When Ruffy saw I was tied up, he came out and I tried a jump pass, but Boogie knocked it away to their other guard. He scooped it up and broke to the basket ahead of Ernie. I cut him off at the foul line, but he hit Boogie with a bounce pass for the deuce.

A press is good if you can stop the ball most of the time. Bryant couldn't. Sky and Tomas helped out bringing the ball down, and their men couldn't stay with them as they got passes just inside the half-court line and dished off to either me or Ernie crisscrossing through the backcourt.

Tomas's man was big and was hacking him to death, but the ref wasn't calling it. I kept thinking about how Tomas was playing and kept telling myself to worry about what *I* was doing. I got the ball in to Tomas low twice, and the first time he threw up a ball that bounced off the rim, only he got his own bound and pushed it up again—it looked goofy but it went in. The second time I threw it in to Tomas on a low roll, his man bumped him and we got the foul call.

What that did was get Boogie's attention to their

inside game. He was running the team from the floor. He started pushing his defense deeper into the paint, but that opened up the outside. I hit a three-pointer from the side. We threw up a surprise full-court press, but Ruffy blew his coverage and left their center wide open under their basket. Their two guard got excited and threw the ball all the way downcourt, over their center's head and out-of-bounds.

"That's the way I planned it," Ruffy said.

I looked over to where House was standing with his hands on his hips wondering what was going on.

A few minutes later, when Sky was on the foul line, House put Colin in for me. Boogie switched to Ernie on defense, and the game suddenly got sloppy. Colin tried to put a move on his man and walked. They brought the ball down and their man stepped on the sideline.

Colin was trying to get into the game but couldn't pick up the rhythm. Ruffy threw up a hook that bounced off the rim. Sky grabbed the bound, almost got tied up in the paint, and then dribbled out. He handed the ball off to Colin, who went straight up for the jumper. Sky's man switched, went up, and caught Colin's shot in the air. It was a sweet move. They got the ball downcourt in a hurry and made an easy deuce.

House put me back in, and I brought the ball down against Boogie. Boogie kept putting his hand on my waist and was squeezing hard, but it didn't look like he was doing anything. The referee started a close-guarding count on me, and Ernie's man came over to double-team me—a mistake—and I hit Ernie at the top of the key. He buried the trey and they called time-out. I saw their coach yelling at the two guard. The game started again, and we exchanged turnovers. Then Ruffy went to the line when he was fouled on a shot at the buzzer. He made the two shots, and I saw we had outscored Bryant 17–12 in the quarter to bring the halftime score to 35–27.

Everybody in the locker room was saying the same thing—that the game wasn't over and we had to stay focused. We were looking good and feeling good. House said that we could take the game away from them in the first few minutes of the second half.

"They have to find their fire," he said. "If they want to win, they have to come out and show it right away. If we come out the way we can, playing solid, aggressive ball, it's our game."

Mr. Barker came to the locker room and said he was proud of us.

I got some alone time and thought about the situation. If we got into the regionals, showed the world what we could do against top competition, I had a chance to cop all my dreams. Sixteen minutes to go and I was pushing onto some heavy reality.

We hit the floor for the second half and I looked around the gym. Jocelyn was there, waving and holding up my number on a large piece of oak tag. Pop was sitting next to her, which surprised me. He pointed at me with both index fingers and grinned.

A tall white woman stopped me on the sideline and asked my name. She was carrying a pad on a clipboard.

"Lawson," I said. "Andrew Lawson."

She looked me up and down as if she was thinking about buying me. "Six-five," she announced, and wrote something down on her pad.

We ran some layups, and House told us not to forget to hustle. We were about to go onto the floor when Fletch asked what the lady had said to me.

"Nothing, really," I said. "She just told me I was

six-five, as if I didn't know it, and wrote something down."

"She's a freelance college scout," Fletch said. "She goes around and makes reports and sells them to the colleges. Don't worry about who's watching you. Just keep your head in the game."

Bryant brought in a new guard, and he was holding me while Boogie was holding Ernie. They were playing a box and one with the one on me, which I didn't understand because our team scoring was spread pretty good over all the starters. Then I found out they were really using a box and beat down. The sucker was hitting me every time I moved.

One time I picked up a loose ball from under their basket and flew downcourt on a two-on-one with Sky. I came down on the beater, did a semispin move in the lane, and fed Sky a soft alley-oop. I put the ball up, then watched Sky fly through the air and slam it down with one hand just as I felt an elbow hit my ribs. I doubled over in pain, but I didn't get a call.

What I did get was pissed. I looked at the referee and he looked back, daring me to open my mouth. I cooled off and smiled.

The next time I got the ball, I hit a three from the corner; then, when Ruffy slapped a pass away, I got the ball, did a give-and-go with Needham, who had just come in the game, and hit a reverse layup a half step in front of Boogie. They called time out and we sat. The cold water and lemon felt good going down.

Both teams were playing team ball, giving everybody on both squads a touch, but we were doing it better. The game was exciting, and at the end of the third quarter the count was 54–41.

We scored the first six points of the fourth quarter to go up 60–41. They called another time-out, and I saw some of the kids from Bryant headed for the doors. That made me feel good.

After the time-out, Boogie brought the ball down. He spread the team out to go one-on-one with me. I was ready for him. He came in hard to my left side and put a spin move back to the center of the court, then a shoulder fake that got me flat on my feet as he went up for a short jumper. The ball didn't touch anything but net. I looked at Boogie to see if he was smiling. He wasn't.

We got the ball, moved up the floor, and got it inside, but Bryant took the ball from Tomas under our hoop. He was fouled but the refs didn't call it. Bryant came down and Boogie buried a three. On our possession we got the ball in to Ruffy, and their center blocked his little jump hook. Boogie grabbed the ball and Ernie chased him, but it didn't do any good. We turned it over on the inbounds play and they scored another deuce and got the foul shot.

Boogie was all over me. He was taking me out of the game, and I felt like crap when Sky turned the ball over on a hesitation walk and their center threw up a shot from the paint that rolled in.

We had started the half comfortable and soon we were looking at the clock, wondering why the quarter was taking so long. They were down by seven. Then they were down by four with a minute and three seconds left. House called a time-out.

"Just hold on to the freaking ball!" he said. "It's a two-possession lead. You hold on to the ball for twenty seconds and they'll have to start fouling."

I passed the ball in to Ernie, who took it across the midcourt line.

Ernie normally loves to handle the ball, but he saw that Sky was open along the baseline and tried to hit him with it. Their whole team saw the pass coming and fought each other to snatch it. They were downcourt in a heartbeat, with Boogie blowing the short jumper but their center putting it back in over Ruffy.

There were thirty-one seconds to go. Ernie picked the ball up to inbound it. He looked for me, saw Boogie coming over, and started to pass the ball to Sky just as he turned away, thinking the ball was coming to me. Ernie held on to the ball but stepped inbounds for a violation and they had the ball back with the same thirty-one seconds.

We tightened our defense, and Boogie had to run out past the top of the key to get the inbounds pass. The moment he touched the ball, he had it on the floor and was driving to his right, running me into a pick set by Sky's man. Sky switched off nicely and went after Boogie. Boogie went up and held the ball until Sky passed him, then threw it softly against the backboard. Meanwhile Ruffy came over and laid a big forearm on Boogie.

The ball rolled in for the deuce and the ref blew the whistle. The score was tied and Boogie was on the line.

There was a commotion near the door, and

I looked and saw that all the Bryant people were coming back. When Boogie sank the free throw, the place went crazy. Bryant was up by a point. I looked up at the clock. There were twenty-six seconds left. House called a time-out.

"We need two! We need two!" he called as we got over to the bench. He was dripping sweat. "Drew brings the ball up quick. When Drew gets to the three-point line, Ruffy comes out to the middle of the lane and Sky comes out to the foul line. Drew, you make a move left and then try to run somebody into a pick. If the pick doesn't work, then Sky, you break out for the short jumper and Tomas and Ruffy get in position for the rebound. Ernie, if we miss and they get the rebound, you foul right away. Got it? Everybody knows what they're supposed to do? It's the three play with Ernie laying back. Everybody got that?"

When we got back on the court, Boogie was in but they had switched the other guard to this tall skinny dude I had seen down at the projects. He was thin but he could leap. Ernie inbounded to me, and Boogie and the tall guy came after me. I passed the ball back to Ernie, and the tall guy went after him while Boogie stayed on my case.

We got the ball downcourt and nobody moved into the right position. Tomas was standing on the right side with his mouth open and Sky had drifted out to the side of the foul line. Ernie saw the play wasn't going to work so he threw the ball in to Ruffy, who shuffled his feet—he could have been called for walking—and then passed out to one side to Sky. Sky dribbled toward me, and Boogie faked as if he was going to double-team him and he passed the ball high to me. Boogie just missed picking it off. I didn't know what the time was but I knew it was going to be close. Boogie had his arms up and I tried a stutter step left, then a full step, and then made a big move as close to his body as I could. I got the half step I wanted and saw their center coming. I went up as hard as I could and all I saw was Boogie's uniform rising with me and Tomas getting some separation behind him. I pumped the ball, and Boogie was reaching for it when I brought it down and behind my back. I could feel Boogie's body against mine, twisting in midair to stop the ball.

Boogie's hand came across my wrist as their center brought two huge hands toward my face. I felt myself falling backward, but I could see, through a forest of arms and hands and frantic fingers, Tomas higher than I had ever seen him and the ball ripping through the net. Ernie had dropped to his knees at the foul line and was screaming. I couldn't hear what he was saying, but the joy in his face told me everything. We had won!

Tomas had made the basket; the final score was 70–69.

House was slapping Tomas on the back. I got up off the floor and tried to get my breathing back to normal again as I walked toward the bench.

Needham ran over and gave me a high five, and so did Abdul.

"You're a player, Lawson!" a voice next to me said. I looked down, and a short, round guy with curly hair was looking up at me. "You still living in Harlem?"

"I know you?" I asked the guy.

"You will," he said, and walked away.

Boogie came over and put his arm around me. "Sweet game, man," he said. "Sweet game."

It was, too.

Everybody plays everybody. Six games in all. If there are only four teams, it means there are six possible wins," Jocelyn said. She was scribbling like crazy on a long yellow pad. "Three teams can win 2 and lose 1. Or two teams can win 2 and lose 1 and two teams can lose 2 and win 1. However, if one team wins 3 games, it's all over because no other team can win more than 2 games. You want to see the math?"

"No."

There were supposed to be five teams in the regionals, but Trinity dropped out at the last minute, leaving Our Lady of Mercy, Roosevelt Academy, Lane, and us. The whole school was going ape, and even dudes who didn't play ball at all were walking around talking about the game.

At practice in the afternoon the guys on the team were told that we would each get four tickets to every game, but we could get more if we wanted them. Sky said he needed at least ten for all his women. Abdul said that Sky could have his tickets because his family didn't know a thing about basketball.

House was trying to act cool, but he wasn't. Only the top team was going on from the regionals to the state finals in Albany, and I knew he was already thinking about it. I was, too. The longer we played, the better chance I would have at getting a dynamite scholarship.

I was looking for a Division I school because that was the way to the pros. You didn't see guys from Division II schools being drafted.

"You could be drafted from a Division II if the right scout or coach saw you play." Fletch and I were sitting on the sidelines watching the team play horse after the workout. "They want more size from a Division II player, though."

"Why?"

"Because they figure if you're playing with a Division I school and you had any playing time, your stats will tell them if you can play or not. Stats don't mean as much in Division II ball."

"They looking for white ballplayers?" I asked, watching Tomas dribble across the foul line, stop short, and throw up a jumper that bounced off the rim.

"If it's a predominantly white school, they are," Fletch said. "If you were scouting for Duke or North Carolina or Kentucky, wouldn't you be looking for white ballplayers?"

"You think that's right?"

"You didn't answer my question." Fletch sniffed twice, then took his handkerchief out of his pocket and blew his nose. "So would you be looking for white players?"

"I guess so."

"Hey, you're finally learning the game," Fletch said. "Next week I'll teach you how to dribble."

House had us working on defense.

"I want you to stop the ball as soon as you can," he said. "We don't want to let a man *walk* the ball upcourt, *walk* across the midcourt line, and set up plays as if he was playing a half-court game."

The way House wanted us playing it was that both guards worked at stopping the ball and then getting back into a loose zone. Ernie and I were the best at doing it, and we felt good with it.

On the way out of the gym after practice I saw a bald-headed black man and a young white man talking to Tomas. I figured they were scouts. Maybe they weren't, but I was checking out everything and letting my mind run wild.

I could understand them looking for white ballplayers. I saw on television that some entire college teams, even the benchwarmers, were black.

When I got home, I was really up. Pops was going through the newspaper and talking about buying a used car. I asked him if he was going to come out to Nassau Coliseum to see any of the games.

"Yeah, I can see me out at the Coliseum," he said. "Maybe you guys can warm up with a pro team."

I didn't think that was going to happen, but I still let myself dream about some pro scouts digging my game.

. . .

So it's Saturday and we're in the deeply righteous locker room at the Coliseum and House is explaining everything to us. "We win all our games, we move to the next level," House said. "It's as simple as that."

We had a game in the morning and a game in the afternoon. Then a game on Sunday either in the morning or afternoon, depending on what the other teams were doing.

Our first game was against Our Lady of Mercy.

Our Lady of Mercy was a big Catholic school on the northern edge of the Bronx. They must have had money's mama, because they came in really fine blue-and-gray buses. We came in the yellow city school bus. When we got on the floor to warm up, we saw they had dynamite satin sweats. They had a bunch of white cheerleaders from a girls' school, and they were looking generally correct.

The game ball felt a little hard, but it bounced okay. It also had slightly raised sections so you could feel where the lines were.

There were a quadrillion people in the stands and guys selling hot dogs and sodas. They had huge televisions above us, and every once in a while I could see myself as we warmed up. It was awesome.

When the game started, it felt funny. We were playing okay and so were they, but somehow it didn't seem real. It was almost as if we were just going through the motions. House and Fletch saw it, too, and started yelling at us.

"You just come out here for the ride?" House asked. We were sitting on the bench during a time-out. "Because I don't think you came to play."

I didn't know if it was where we were playing or what. I knew the place was huge, and it made me feel smaller. It was as if the size of the place were taking away my strength. Ruffy wasn't doing much at center and nobody was picking up the slack. There wasn't any excitement in the game, no fire. After the time-out I could feel the team hustling more, but at halftime we were down by five, 39–34.

The second half started with them hitting two treys in a row. One was by my man and House yanked me. I thought he was getting frustrated. Ricky and Ernie were in the backcourt. From the sideline I could see what was shaking. They were snatching the boards big-time over Tomas and Sky. Ruffy got a few boards, but he wasn't getting enough to get us back into the game. Tomas was doing okay on offense, and I saw that his game looked tighter than I thought it had been.

"Yo, coach, put me back in!" I knelt down in front of House. "I can bring us back."

House nodded toward the scorer's table, and I went and checked in. When Ruffy fouled one of their guards, I came in for Ricky. They weren't in the bonus yet and brought the ball in from the sideline. I found my man and just started pushing him around the court.

The brother I was holding was about six feet and an okay ballplayer. He was thin and dark-skinned, and he had a few nice moves but set up plays more than he shot unless he was wide open. I pushed him away from the sideline, putting my body against him and leaning with my hand on his waist.

They brought the ball in and set up a pick behind the foul line in front of the key. Their forward came out, ran Ruffy into the pick, and took the J. The ball bounced off the rim and straight up. I went in from the side of the lane and grabbed the ball. Our guys started downcourt. I handed the ball off to Ernie.

"We're not blocking out," I said to him. "They're getting up in the air with no fight."

I went downcourt and started yelling at the guys to block out under the boards. I didn't care if the other team heard me, because I figured we were stronger than they were. None of them had any real size and they weren't even close to cut.

I knew blocking out strong would get us back into the game. For some reason we were just standing up straight and jumping for the rebounds when we needed to be leaning on some bodies. Ruffy started to catch fire and use his big body and strength to dominate.

We started controlling both boards. I fed Tomas and he worked the moves that Fletch had shown him, hitting four shots in a row.

The mo changed big-time and their coach called a time-out.

"He's going over to the refs, asking for fouls," Fletch said.

House saw their coach talking with his palms up, copping a plea. House went over to talk for us.

"Keep feeding Tomas inside!" I said.

"He's playing too deep! He's playing too deep!" Ruffy wanted Tomas to get away from right under the basket.

Tomas was good under there because he collected all the garbage and went right back up on offense and held on to the ball on the defensive boards. But Ruffy was right. He had to come out some, because it was taking too long to set up our stuff with him being in too deep.

When we were on the court again, I talked to Tomas.

"Come out a step, maybe two," I said.

"Don't tell me how to play," he came back.

"If we lose, I'm going to punch you in your face after the game," I said.

He gave me a look, but he moved outside a little. And I figured him to be a better player when he was mad.

The ref started calling fouls on us but that was okay, because we didn't have any from the first half so nobody was in trouble. We caught Mercy with three minutes to go. Then they just folded, whining to the refs about how we were pushing them and fouling them. We were pushing and there were a few fouls that weren't being called, but they were using that as an excuse to lose the game. Good.

The game ended 68–64.

House said something stupid about us finally learning the game. Fletch came over and gave everybody five. He didn't have to say anything else.

Relax. Everybody was talking about relaxing, but we were all up way too high.

"This is big-time, man! This is big-time!" Ernie was running around the locker room, scoping out the rubbing tables, refrigerators filled with soft drinks and water, and whatever else he could get into.

House got us together after a while, and we went out for lunch. Some people in the restaurant were looking at us, and a kid came over and asked us were we the Nets from the NBA.

"The Nets can't play with us," Abdul said. "We're too good."

The kid gave Abdul a look that said he didn't believe a word he was saying, but he still asked him for his autograph.

Then everybody was talking about why the kid had picked Abdul to talk to and get his autograph. Abdul said it was because he was a Muslim and his inner beauty was shining through.

"Even kids recognize what a beautiful person I am," he added.

We finished our lunch and went for a walk, with House and Fletch guarding us like we were precious. I dug that. We were all feeling good, but we had another game coming up.

Roosevelt didn't have as many fans as Our Lady of Mercy and hardly any white folks, but the bunch of kids who did come were noisy. They brought only eight players—all wide dudes who looked like they should have been digging ditches or something. They all wore do-rags during warm-ups, which I thought was tough, and they were joking around like they had already copped the win.

"Whatever game you got, you have to leave it on the floor today," House said. "We don't want to lose because we didn't put out."

When we lined up, my man put his fist up and I hit it. He tried to hold it firm and show off his manhood. The sucker was cut, but he looked a little funny because he had a long body and short legs. He was my height, though, and I figured him to be strong. The way it turned out, he wasn't just strong, he was like King Kong's little brother. I expected the dude to start pounding his chest and going chee-chee-chee or something.

They won the tap and brought the ball down, and my man took me in deep and called for the ball. When he got it, he started backing me in toward the basket, and I knew he was stronger than me. I held him out the best I could, waiting for some help. Tomas came over and King Kong went up and blew the layup. As he came down, I boxed him out and got the bound.

I passed out to Ernie and we came downcourt fast. Ernie's man stopped the ball, and Ernie passed it to me. I saw Tomas open on the left side and got the ball to him on a bounce as he moved, and he made the easy deuce.

Their starting five were all big, all strong, but they didn't know a thing about playing ball. On defense they were in a loose zone and just beat on whoever was near them. It got so bad that the refs were calling only the worst fouls. It was like in the school yard—no blood, no foul. On offense it was like they had never been in a gym before. Whoever had the ball did his thing, and everybody else just stood around. Man on man they were good. They were real good. They moved well, they could leap, almost fly through the air. They had good hands, great bodies. At any moment they had five brothers with dynamite reflexes and bitching nice moves on the wood, but you can't beat a team going one against five.

At the end of the half we were up by eleven and it wasn't even that close. House said they would get their game together in the second half, but I didn't think so. The way they were playing, rapping and joking around with each other, it was as if they didn't know what was going on.

I wanted to win bad, but I felt like I should have stopped the game and asked those brothers if they knew what kind of game they were in. We were on the court living out our lives. I was playing my heart out, trying to get over—what were they doing? Had they been fooled? Did they think that the game was going to do for them whatever they wanted? That it didn't matter how they played as long as they performed the way they wanted? When House took me out at the end of the third quarter, I mentioned that Roosevelt didn't seem serious.

He shrugged. It didn't matter to him. He was

looking for a win for us, for himself. What the guys on Roosevelt were doing was off the screen.

The way Roosevelt played bothered me. I wanted the win as much as House did, as much as anybody did, but the fact that brothers were goofing when they had business to take care of was just wrong.

I played more. It was my game and Tomas's game and Sky's game and the team's game. Everything we had done in practice came in. We ran backdoor plays, overloads, and trey kickouts until we were tired. When House took me out again, he pointed up at the score clock. We had 70 to their 58 with fifteen seconds to go. I flopped down on the bench and took the water some girl was handing me. I didn't drink it, just held it in my hands with my legs stretched out in front of me.

"How you feeling?" Fletch called over to me. He was wearing the biggest smile I had ever seen on him.

"I feel good."

Mom had floured some chicken in the morning, and when we got home, she deep-fried it and we had it along with some homemade French fries and green peas.

"Everybody was just looking at you and hanging on everything you did!" Mom said. "You don't know how proud of you I was."

"Didn't I tell you that Drew is the man?" Jocelyn had a chicken wing in her hand as she talked. "When he came out on the court for the second half, I could see he was going to take care of business. What did you think, Pops?"

"He was okay," Pops said.

"What you mean, *okay*?" Mom put her hands on the tops of her thighs. "You think he was just *okay*?"

"Drew, I don't know that much about ball playing," Pops said. "But I was sitting in the stands and watching all the people watching you, and it was like . . . a real good feeling. You did some play and this man sitting next to me got all excited . . ."

Pops started tearing up.

"You okay, Pops?" Jocelyn asked.

"Yeah, I'm okay," Pops said. "You know, I never had nothing like that in my life. People cheering. Some people cheering for the other team. What you were doing was important. I was thinking about you going to college and all, and it means a lot to me. You being my boy and all."

"How about me?" Jocelyn asked. "I don't count because I'm a girl?"

"No, you count, honey," Pops said. "But—you know, you're smart and everything."

"Yo, you mean I'm not smart enough to go to college?" I put on a mean face.

Pops looked at me and started to say something,

but then he got choked up and just gave my arm a little push.

After supper I went to my room and called Ruffy. His mom said he was in the bathroom and he'd call me back. I had just hung up when Jocelyn knocked and, before I could tell her to come in, had framed herself in the doorway.

"You want me to stand here and adore you or anything?" she asked.

"Hey, you're looking pretty good today," I said.

"Yes, I know. As soon as you go off to college, all the boys are going to be chasing me like anything," she said. "I'm going to be like a defenseless little girl running across the ice to the promised land, and they'll be after me like those mean old hounds, sniffing out my beautiful self."

"You know, you really ought to take some self-confidence lessons," I said.

"If you feel as good as you look like you're feeling, you ought to put it in a bottle or something and sell it on eBay," she said.

"I feel like going outside and telling everybody about the games."

"So why don't you?" Jocelyn's eyebrows came

together. "They need to hear some good news in this neighborhood."

I felt a little stupid taking the elevator downstairs just to tell somebody how good I felt, but I did anyway. There were two guys on the stoop, but I didn't know them. One of them looked sleepy, or maybe even high. Just seeing him started me coming down off my good feeling.

"Yo, Blood, I got them CDs you been looking for, man," he said. "I got some DVDs, two smoking iPods, and a whole lot of watches. What you need today?"

"I'm good," I said. "Don't need nothing."

"You know I ain't selling nothing but some bargains," the guy said. "All the latest jams . . ."

"No, I'm good," I said again.

The dude nodded, and he and his boy stepped down from the stoop and started up the street. The tax-preparing place hadn't been open for a week, and the guys standing in front of it had started a small fire in a trash can. It wasn't that cold, but there was a slight chill in the air.

The two guys from the stoop stopped to talk with the others, and I watched as they showed them the CDs and stuff they were selling.

What I wished was that they were all into playing ball and wanted to hear about how Baldwin had won the games and how well I thought I had done. But that wasn't what was going down. What they were doing was getting on with their lives, dealing with the corner business, dealing with whatever they had to sell or buy on their market to get money for whatever they needed to be doing, or thought they needed to be doing, with their lives.

In a way it was like a bunch of guys in a game. They were falling behind every minute that passed, but they had lost interest in the score. It was as if they were just a ton behind and had given up on the win. And maybe deep inside they didn't want to peep the score, maybe they knew what was happening but just didn't want to think about it anymore. I could understand that. I had played enough ball in my life, and was deep enough into my game to know I had to be in the hunt for a win or I could lose who I was. And once I lost who I was, my inner me, then all the CDs and all the iPods and all the bling in the world wasn't going to make it right.

The strange thing was that everybody was feeling

the same thing, that there was a huge game going on, and that the game was going to decide who was a winner and who lost. But so many of the brothers on the corner didn't have a play. They were out buying their uniforms, their gold chains, and the fancy clothes like they were real players, but they knew better. Even when they angled into their best gangster lean, it was just a pose. There was never going to be a jump ball. I could feel for them because they were just like me in most ways, thinking that everybody should have a number, everybody should have the same playing time, and knowing it wasn't going to happen.

I thought about Tony. I wondered—when he was sitting in his room at night, in the darkness and alone with his thoughts, did he think he still had a win? I wondered if he thought back to the time when he was playing ball and thought about what might have been. People checking out Tony, the lawyers, the police, all figured he had just blown his chance. The game had been on the line and he had been all by himself and blown the layup. But for most of the people in the hood it wasn't like that at all. It was about the mystery of the game and not figuring out the rules until it was too late to cop the W and too late for the big comeback.

When we got to the arena the next day for the final playoff game, I was about as nervous as I could get. To make it worse, there was a television crew there and a whole section of photographers. Tomas's mother had come, and she stood up and waved to me. Across from the television cameras there was a big banner that spelled out L-A-N-E.

Everybody knew Franklin K. Lane High School. Little kids in Brooklyn who wanted to play ball would hang around their school yard to show off their stuff. You had to play good team ball to stay with their squad, and you always had to look over your shoulder to see who was sneaking up on your position. I had even thought of going there, but Ruffy didn't want to play in Brooklyn and both of us had wanted to play at the same school that Tony had done his thing in.

"There aren't any dragons on their team," House said. "Nobody who's going to eat us up. But every player on their team has talent, and we're going to have to play both ways—offense and defense—if we're going to walk away with the championship. Nobody brought us here but our own efforts. Hard work and talent got us here, and it can take us to the next level. So let's get it done!"

When the teams came out, the refs had us all shake hands. The dude I was up against had fat clammy hands. He was younger than me, but he was big.

Ernie got the tap, brought the ball up to the midcourt line, and got double-teamed right away. I came over, got a jump pass, and made a quick move to the basket. My man stayed with me as I passed the key, but he didn't react when I dished the ball in to Ruffy deep. Ruffy took the ball up, got away with a push-off, and made the deuce.

Their point guard brought the ball down really fast, and our guys were hustling to get back. My man ran me into a pick, but I recovered and got to him. The ball came in to the man who had picked me, and he made an easy two.

We brought the ball down again, with them stopping the ball really high. We ran a play along the baseline with Ruffy trying to pick Tomas's man, but their center slowed Tomas down with an elbow and then stole the pass when Ernie tried to hit Ruffy again. Okay, they were sharp.

The Lane players were flat-out good. They played like they were going to business. All they needed were some attaché cases.

At the quarter they were ahead 19–14. Fletch said they had used nine guys in the first quarter.

"They're outhustling us on offense," House said. "They're bringing the ball down faster than any team we've faced. On defense they're solid, but nothing special. We need to tighten up our defense and keep them off the boards."

I hadn't thought much about the boards, but we were only getting one shot most of the time.

Ernie hit a trey to start the second quarter, and when they got a backcourt violation, he hit another one. We were up by a point, but they came back and started the same routine.

"Come on, let's get it going! Let's get it going!" Abdul had come in to give Sky a breather and was trying to pump things up.

I remembered the last game. I wanted to take it on my shoulders, but I didn't want to showboat or nothing. I went after my man hard on D, ragging him wherever he went. I pushed him when I caught him standing still, and talked to him whenever he got the ball.

"Give it up, fool! Give it up!"

He looked at me like I was crazy, and one of their players, a forward, told me to keep my mouth shut.

"Why don't you come and shut it?"

The next time I got the ball, he came up on me too close and I brought the ball between my legs, faked putting it through his, and when he took a half step back, I made a move toward the basket. I got a step on him, but the other guard cut me off. I moved between them, and when my man tried to recover with a lunge in front, I dished it out to Ernie.

Ernie got tied up by their forward and moved the pill outside to set it up again. We had penetrated, but we hadn't scored. I knew it was going to be a long game.

When we stepped up our game, we were playing them just about even. We took away the little bump-and-run pick they were using and hustled back on defense fast enough to keep them from setting up easy plays. They had only one fast break the whole second quarter. But at the end of the half they were still ahead, 36–29.

"Right now it's anybody's game," House was saying in the locker room. "Whoever wants it the most is going to get it. How much you guys want it? How much you guys want it?"

We all said we wanted it more than Lane did, and we meant it. Seven points can disappear in a heartbeat, and I knew it and everybody on both teams knew it.

We came out and started our warm-ups for the second half. When a television reporter started talking to the two coaches, I went over to where Fletch was standing.

"What you thinking?" I asked him.

"They're not turning the ball over," he said. "We got to take it on defense and get the ball inside more on offense. Their guards keep double-teaming the ball, and that boy on you is holding you so tight, I thought he was part of your jersey."

The third quarter was all them. They didn't do anything special, but they made plays and all we could get were a few humbles and some lucky bounces. At the end of the quarter they were up by nine.

"Tomas, can you do anything inside, man?" I asked him as we went out for the last quarter.

"Get me the ball," he said.

He didn't say it with a lot of confidence, but I saw that me and Ernie weren't killing their guards. House wanted to win too bad to bring Colin in, and Ricky was too small to deal with their big guards. Sky's man was tall, and he had this little twelve-foot jumper that he hit anytime Sky gave him an inch. Sky could keep him away from that shot, but he was keeping Sky off the boards. Tomas couldn't jump with their forwards, so that left all the rebounding to Ruffy and whatever came out to me and Ernie.

"If you get the trey, take it," House called to me.

It had worked the day before, but the man holding me wasn't giving up squat.

Lane hardly ever made mistakes, but they started the fourth quarter with a weak turnover when their two guard carried the ball. On our possession I made a nice move at the top of the key and hit Tomas sliding across the lane. He got the ball and went up in one motion, made the deuce, and got the foul.

Tomas made the foul shot. Lane brought the ball down slowly, which surprised me. I thought they might be thinking about sitting on their lead, even though it was down some. They weren't. What they did was spread their offense, bring out the new forward, and try to isolate him on Tomas. The forward they were using was shorter than Tomas, but he handled the ball well. He made a move on Tomas, spun around him, and walked the ball inside. The refs didn't whistle the carry and the play made Tomas look bad.

"Drew! Drew! Twenty-three switch! Twenty-three switch!" House was screaming from the sideline.

We turned it over and fell back on defense. I switched defensive assignments with Tomas, who was our number 23, and he came out and took the young guard.

The forward I had mouthed off to told the new guy to burn me. He put the ball on the floor, threw a shoulder fake, and then made a quick move to go around me. But he was going too wide, and I stayed with him. I was on him when he went up, and when he let the ball go rim high, I pinned it against the boards, then knocked it out toward Sky. When Sky went coast to coast and slammed, everybody on our bench was on their feet.

The Lane coach, a short little brown-skinned dude, ran halfway up the floor calling the next play. They brought the ball down again, gave it to the same forward—who threw a jive fake inside that couldn't have fooled a Barbie doll—and came across the center.

"Pick left!" Ruffy called it.

I knew it was coming and slammed an elbow into the dark body to my left. It was the same pick-and-run play they had made in the first quarter, where the guy who set the pick took the contact and then peeled to the basket. When I saw Sky pick up my man, I moved with the other forward as he reached for the ball. He should have gone straight up, but he bounced the ball once and dipped his knees. I knew he wanted to slam and I went up with him, reaching over his head and putting my fingers on the top of the ball before he started his dunk.

The dude was strong, but so was I, and I was on top of the ball so there was nothing he could do. As we came down together, I heard the whistle blow and saw the ref's hands go up for the jump ball.

Yeah!

He tried to cop a plea for a foul, but the play was too pretty to be whistling any lame fouls. I had just embarrassed the chump and everybody knew it.

I had a good feeling in my stomach. We were going to win.

We hit some quick buckets and they got sloppy. They were still working plays, but they weren't crisp.

Time was flying, and when the ref stopped play to wipe some sweat off the court, I checked the clock. There were less than two minutes to play and we were actually up by a point. House called a time-out. He told us what the deal was.

"We need to score a deuce and then be aggressive to get the ball back," he said. "What they need to do is get the ball now. They know that and you know that, so hang on to the ball and look for a good shot. Sky, get more active. See if you can shake your man without the ball, then go for the backdoor. Drew, Ernie, if you see Sky break loose, see what it creates. It could end up with a backdoor or the two play, with both of you coming in and crossing at the foul line. Stay alert. It's our game if we want it!"

Time was back in and the game was on. This was my game. I felt it, I could almost taste it as Ernie passed to me.

I put the ball on the floor and went hard to my right. As I moved toward the key, I saw Sky's man chasing him. Tomas blocked out Sky's man, and I let the pass go. Sky made the deuce and we were up by three. I looked up and there were thirty seconds to go.

House was waving us into a full-court press. I found my man and got on him as their center inbounded a full-court pass. I looked downcourt and saw Ernie chasing his man. The ball landed in the lane, and the dude who got it swooped it up and made a perfect layup. They had scored in one second.

We were still up by one, and now it was Lane who was in the full-court press. We got the ball across the ten-second line and they weren't sure what to do. They made a few attempts at the ball but they didn't want to foul us.

I didn't want to look at the clock but I did. Fifteen seconds.

"Foul him! Foul him!" their coach was screaming.

My man came toward me, and so did Ernie's man. I passed the ball to Ernie, who was open. They both ran toward him and he passed it to Sky, who started in one direction, then changed his mind and walked with the ball.

The ref blew his whistle as he signaled the walking violation.

I looked up at the clock. Six seconds. Their ball.

They called a time-out. They had six seconds to do something with the ball. We had six seconds to stop them.

"Okay, okay!" House was down on one knee in front of us. "We don't have to worry about fouling them. I don't think the ref is going to give them the game on the line. We don't foul intentionally, but we're aggressive after the ball. We reach for leather! We reach for leather! On three!"

"One! Two! Three!"

We lined up close. It was jersey on jersey, sweat on sweat. They were in a tight line when the ref threw the ball to them. Their center backed off, and their two guards took off down the court. Me and Ernie chased them and caught them before they turned. We turned with them and saw one of their forwards with the ball. I knew he was the one who had made the short jumpers. My man came out and took a bounce pass, with me reaching for the ball. He started falling forward. I brought my hands back and saw him push the ball back to the guy who had brought the ball down. Sky was still on him when he faked a move at the foul line and went straight up. Sky went up with him and they seemed to go up forever. The ball left the dude's fingertips, and I turned and looked for somebody to block out. I saw their center move toward the basket and I stepped in front of him. I felt him on my back as the ball came down, rattled around the rim, and fell through as the buzzer sounded.

My head went crazy. I looked around for the scoreboard. At first I couldn't find it high above the stands. Then I saw it, but by that time I didn't need it. All the Lane players were screaming and shouting around me. We had lost.

In the locker room Sky was sobbing in the corner. Nobody thought it was his fault, nobody thought that he had lost the game or even that his mistake had cost us the game. But nobody had the emotional energy to console him. I was numb; all my tears were inside.

The world stopped. It just stopped. Noises stopped. Movement stopped. Reasons stopped happening. Someone was trying to get us to go back out onto the floor for some kind of ceremony. People were patting us on the back. Words were coming at us. But my world had stopped.

Was the game too important in my life? Did it weigh too much for me to carry any farther? I didn't know. I just knew I felt so miserable. It was as if standing in the locker room, trying to get up the courage to go through the doors into the corridor and onto the gym floor again, was the moment that summed up my whole life.

We stood in a line on the floor and were given watches. There were photos and congratulations. Then we were back in the locker room and changing our clothes.

Jocelyn and Mom were in the parking lot. Jocelyn's eyes were red despite her smile. Mom was patting me on the shoulder, her lips saying something I couldn't hear or maybe couldn't understand.

How quiet can a bus be?

House was cool. He went to each guy on the team, even the ones who had sat on the bench for the whole game, and said something about how the year had gone or what he hoped for next year.

Monday came, and there was a special assembly to thank us.

"We need to thank the team for their athletic performances," Mr. Barker said. "But we also need to thank them for how they represented Baldwin. They were gentlemen in their wins, and gentlemen in their one defeat. I was proud of all of them, and proud of the school they come from."

There was excitement about the NCAA college tournament. People were picking favorites, still high on the momentum of our tournament. I watched part of it, but I wasn't really into it.

The team still hung together. Tomas was the first one to get college offers. He got an offer from New Mexico, one from West Virginia, and one from Winona State. We helped him look up Winona and found it was in Minnesota. They were a Division II school. I congratulated Tomas, but I felt bad that it was him and not me. I didn't think it was right for me to feel bad, but I did. He said he would talk it over with House to see where he would go.

"The school that is cheapest is the one I will love," he said. "What school are you going to go to?"

"I'm not even sure," I lied, not wanting to say that I hadn't received any offers. "I might even play pro ball in Italy for a while."

Ernie got two offers, one from a university in Puerto Rico and one from Monroe Community College. He took the one at Monroe because he didn't know anything about Puerto Rico.

"If I go to Puerto Rico, they're going to expect me to speak good Spanish, man," he said.

All I could think was that at least he had two offers.

Sky got an offer from Providence, which had a smoking basketball program, and I hadn't figured him to get even a sniff from a Division I school. He said he had been hoping to play ball in the Midwest but that Providence was okay.

"All the fine mamas go to the Midwest schools," he said.

I had sent regular applications to a number of schools, as my guidance counselor had advised me. My first letter back was from Arizona. It was a straight letter turning me down and asking me to reconsider for my sophomore year. Then I was turned down by Howard, in D.C., Charleston Southern, Virginia Union, the University of Washington, and Louisiana State University.

Ruffy didn't get any offers either, and he was talking about working for the Transit Authority.

"Or maybe I'll open a store," he said. "That way I can give Tony a job if he comes up for parole."

I knew Ruffy's mom didn't have any money to open a store, but I let it slide. The funny thing was at least Tony didn't have to worry about what he was doing. That was seriously bad thinking, but I was feeling it.

It wasn't that I just felt bad. I could deal with bad. But I felt ordinary. All my dreams of playing pro ball and being a star looked as if they were gone, and I was going to be just another brother standing on a Harlem street corner, leaning in a ghetto doorway, pretending the street hustle wasn't about me.

Saturday morning I went to play ball but just sat on the bench and watched some kids. When I got home, Jocelyn met me at the door.

"There's a priest here to see you," she said. "Who did you kill today?"

I knew I hadn't done anything and thought something had happened to Tony.

The priest was sitting in the living room, a cup of tea in front of him, looking cool in his priest outfit and white hair. The man with him was familiar. He was the one who had talked to me at the Bryant game, who had said I was a player. He looked a little sleazier sitting in my living room wearing a cheap suit that was getting shiny around the knees. Mom was sitting in the chair near the window. I couldn't figure what was going down, but Jocelyn hadn't given me a heads-up, which she would have if there was something I needed to know.

They stood up when I walked into the room.

"Hello, Drew. I'm Father Gabaccia, and this is Coach Mickey Burns." The priest extended his hand and I shook it.

Burns stood up and looked me up and down. "You're a solid six-five, maybe six-six," he said. "So many kids put down six-something on their résumés and they're really five-something."

"We've come by to leave you with some information about our basketball program at DePaul University," the priest said. "We think you'd fit into our program nicely, and we're offering you a full scholarship if you commit to us. We had some other players in mind along with you, some quite good, but we can't get them all. We've brought along a ton of paper for you to go over, but I just want to add two things. One is that we can offer smaller class sizes than most schools and you'll get all the help you need to succeed academically, and second, we really want you out in Chicago."

"That sounds good to me, sir," I said.

"You were number three on our list of guards," Burns said. "It doesn't mean that you were the third best guard, it was just that we felt that the other two young men had a slightly better fit. We were lucky to get our first two choices. One was a beautiful kid from Chicago. Had everything going for him. Unfortunately he was caught up in a drive-by shooting and was wounded pretty badly. We're going to give him a scholarship if he makes it, even though he probably won't be able to play ball for us. That's how much we think of him."

"If he can't play ball?" I asked.

"Spinal injury," Burns said. "We have high hopes for the second kid. He's a junior college transfer, so he's got some experience on you, but you have size on him. I hope you look over the papers and DVD we brought, and that it will make you want to call us. You'll look great bringing the ball down for DePaul."

I didn't want to grin. I wanted to be so cool, so calm and laid-back, and I almost pulled it off. Then I looked over and saw Mom sitting on the edge of her seat and Jocelyn sitting at the table.

"I've seen you play a number of times," Coach Burns said. "I saw the way you handled yourself against Bryant, and I particularly liked the way you played against Lane. That was a tough team. I thought you could have worked the boards more in the first half. What do you think?"

"They were tough on the boards," I said. "But I should have been in there banging with them."

What DePaul had to offer was a full ride. Coach Burns started telling me about the program, who all they played, and who had played for them in the past.

"If you decide on our program, you're going to have some competition for the starting guard slot," Father Gabaccia said. "But you certainly have size and character going for you."

They left me with some booklets about the school. All I had to do was write a letter of intent and I was set. I told them I would talk it over with my family and let them know as soon as possible.

When they left, me and Mom and Jocelyn were jumping up and down that apartment and hugging each other big-time. I had my tears coming again and couldn't stop them.

House called me at ten thirty. He had heard about the offer, and Fletch called a little while later. He said he was sure he could get me into Armstrong Atlantic.

"Where's that?"

"Savannah, Georgia," Fletch said. "I think it's the best school for you. You go to Armstrong and you can cruise through. You go to DePaul and you'll have to play on national television, everybody in the country will be reading about you, all the pro scouts will be tracking your every move. You wouldn't want that, would you?"

"Yeah, I think I can deal with it," I said. I was smiling, and I knew Fletch was, too. "Yo, Fletch, did you think I was going to get some good offers?"

"There was nothing written in stone, Drew," Fletch said. "You have the skills, but sometimes the ball doesn't bounce the way we want it to, does it?"

"No, man, it sure doesn't."

Later, when I was lying across my bed, just about levitating with joy, Jocelyn came into the room with a bunch of three-by-five index cards.

"Sign these for me and I'll sell them on eBay," she said, tossing the cards on the bed.

I picked them up and tossed them back at her. She sat on the edge of the bed and wiped my face with the palm of her hand.

"You must get that boohoo stuff from Mama,

because she's in there crying her little heart out," she said.

We had what Mr. Barker called Graduate Day, which consisted of some local schools setting up tables in the gym, handing out brochures, and answering questions about financial aid. All seniors had the morning off so we could talk to them if we wanted, and the gym was filled.

"Drew, let's get a soda." Tomas hadn't been hanging out that much, and he had told Ernie that he didn't want to play any ball until he reached college.

We dodged the traffic getting across the street, picked up our sodas at the counter, and settled in a booth.

"How's your mom?" I asked. "She still fighting the system?"

"Most of the time she's talking about me going off to college," Tomas said, trying to straighten his legs out under the table. "I think she misses her college days."

"She's got to be thinking about you going off," I said. "She's going to be home by herself, right?"

"I didn't think about that," he said. "This will be the first time she's been alone in America. Your mother talking about college, too?"

"I'll be the first in the family to go," I said. "But she'll have my pops and little sister home, so she'll be okay."

We talked about what we thought college would be like and making the change from high school. Tomas seemed confident, and I tried to act more confident than I felt.

I wondered if I would ever play against him in college or the pros. In a way I liked him. He had reached out and tried to be friendly. His mom had, too. But I felt that we would never be close enough to hang together, to be real friends. That was okay, too. I didn't need to be close to everybody. Life didn't have the same neat boxes I imagined would be waiting for me. They didn't have them for Tomas or his family, either. He had his game to play out, and I had mine. I thought that he would get better chances than me, more attention, but I had learned something more about the set, and how deep my game could be.

I got two more offers. One of them, Towson State

in Maryland, sent a brochure, and they even had a photograph of me in a Towson State uniform. The magazine was slick and I dug it. A school from Iowa sent a small package of clippings from their local newspaper along with a DVD showing kids sitting around the campus, the ball team, and a really sincere-looking black girl staring into the camera telling me why I should consider their school.

The last part of the DVD was a picture of a clock, ticking off the seconds, and a voice-over.

> *"All eyes are on Lawson as he brings the ball down the left side. He fakes right and then makes a quick move across the middle. Now he stops and goes straight up. The ball is in the air! He scores! He scores!"*

I wanted to go to DePaul so bad I could taste it. Mr. Barker helped me write the letter of intent and laughed when my hand was shaking as I signed it.

House congratulated me, and so did Fletch. When I got a moment with Fletch alone, I apologized for some of the things I had said along the way.

"Drew, your enemies can mess your life up," he said. "Or they can make it easy for you to do it to yourself. You need to congratulate yourself for not blowing your chances. Go on to college, represent the way you're supposed to, and then maybe we can talk about it again one day."

I knew I could represent. I would do it for Mom and Jocelyn, who were going to be in my corner no matter what. I would do it for Pops and all the dreams he had looked at from a distance. I was even representing, in a strange kind of way, for the brother in Chicago who had serious game but who had been cut down in a drive-by.

And somewhere, in a dark part of my mind, I was representing for coach Burns's list of guards. He told me I was number three, but how many guys had been on the list and couldn't deal with the SAT or had messed up their averages? How many would spend the next ten years busting butt on a hundred playgrounds around the country and not getting squat out of it? If I hadn't made it through high school, if I had been arrested or shot up, how many more dudes with serious game could have taken my place? It was something to think about, something to deal with. My moment had come, but I knew that what mattered was what I did with it.

The hardest thing going down was being around Ruffy. I didn't want to think of him standing on the corner waiting for whatever came his way. I thought it would have been different if the thing with Tony hadn't happened. Maybe later Ruffy would be able to go to college. I hoped so. I think he deserved more than he was getting, but so did a lot of people.

But for me the sun was shining, clouds were doing their floating thing, birds were making their little bird circles, and life was kicking. I thought of the brother me and Ruffy had met on the elevator in the court building. "Not guilty."

I was in my room when Jocelyn came to the door, leaned against the jamb, and asked me was I scared to go off to college.

"You can tell me," she said. "I won't tell anyone."

"I'm a little nervous about it," I said.

"And ain't that cool?" she asked.

It was.

EXTRAS

GAME

Walter Dean Myers Dishes on Writing *Game*

Game really delivers the basketball action, so what's the scoop on your latest novel?

Game is a novel about two young men who are in love with basketball, and who see basketball as perhaps their way to success and fame. They are coming from two very different places. Drew comes from Harlem, where I grew up. Tomas is a white ballplayer from Prague. Drew and Tomas find themselves on the same city basketball team, and they have to adjust both to the city game and to each other. Basketball is a great game, but there are aspects about life that they also have to learn.

Drew thinks he is the best player on the team. Why does he still have to learn the coach's system?

It's not so much that he has to be a team player. He's not willing to play with his teammates. But he has to learn a system in which the coach is very much at ease and in which he is very much at ease. So when the coach brings in Tomas, and wants to alter the game so that Tomas is also effective, Drew feels threatened.

Why did you choose a player from Europe?

A lot of ballplayers come into the NBA from Eastern Europe, and these kids have similar backgrounds to many of the young people from the inner cities in the United

States. They are often very poor and struggling to make it, and they have the same basketball dreams. So I thought it would be very interesting to bring in a ballplayer from Prague. It was also a lot of fun to go to Prague and check out the city and the ballplayers there.

In English class, Drew is reading the play *Othello* by Shakespeare. What parallels did you want to make between Drew's life and Othello's life?

The ballplayers, and many teenagers that I know, lead such very, very narrow lives, and they often don't travel outside their neighborhoods. I needed some way that Drew could look beyond his own life. When I was growing up in Harlem, that passageway was literature and books. I was hoping that Drew would look at Othello and Iago, and at least wonder if there was something larger going on.

Did you also want Drew to associate the coach with Iago, the villain?

I hoped he would think about it, and try to figure out whether the coach was a villain or just someone with different needs from Drew's. Also, there is the idea that Drew has to come of age; he has to understand that Tomas's needs were not congruent with his, and neither were the coach's.

Drew figures out that there's more than just winning the game. Do you think the coach knows this, too?

I think the coach sees it. But when you have an excellent ballplayer on your team, at any level—at elementary school, high school, college, or the pros—that ballplayer gives the coach an opportunity as well as the team, and I think that the coach, in this case, was pursuing that opportunity.

In your novel, did you make all the plays up, or are some of them based on the games that you played in?

It's a mix. Some of the plays I made up, and some are from my own playing days, which are now past, and some are from coaching tapes—watching some of the coaches try to bring the flex offense into college and even into high schools.

Well, now that you've brought up your playing days, we need to know what position you played.

When I was in the army, I played the small forward, because I'm only six foot two. When I came out of the army, I played with a very big team. I was the second smallest guy and I played guard. I like guard better.

What do you think basketball means to kids today?

It's an accessible path. Kids see ballplayers who look like they do and talk like they do, and it fulfills their dreams. Even if you tell young ballplayers that their chances of making the pros are very, very remote, they still hope.

Walter Dean Myers's All-Time Starting Five

Guards: Jerry West and Michael Jordan
Forwards: Dave DeBusschere and Julius Erving
Center: Wilt Chamberlain

Walter Dean Myers's Current Starting Five:

Center: Tim Duncan, San Antonio Spurs
Forward: Kevin Garnett, Boston
Forward: Dirk Nowitzki, Dallas
1 Guard: Chris Paul, New Orleans
2 Guard: Gilbert Arenas, Washington

Walter Dean Myers's Favorite Venues for Basketball

Madison Square Garden
The Cage on West 4th Street
Wherever the Rucker tournament is being held

Walter Dean Myers's Favorite Basketball Team

The New York Knicks

EXCERPT FROM

Dope Sick

MY ARM WAS HURTING bad. Real bad. The bone could have been broken. I couldn't tell. I just knew it was hurting and swollen. I felt like just taking the gun out and throwing it away and giving up so I could get the mess over with. I opened my mouth so I wouldn't make so much noise when I breathed. Down the street I saw the patrol car was still at the corner. He had his lights flashing. I didn't know if he'd seen which way I was running or not. I knew I was too tired to keep running much more.

I started to lift my arm to look at my watch and the whole arm just lit up with pain. The bone had to be broken. I figured it was two or three o'clock in the morning. Skeeter had called me just past midnight and told me they got Rico. I knew Rico was going to punk out. In a way I was glad they got him, but I knew he was going to blame everything on me.

I was in the shadows in a shop doorway and I knew I couldn't stay there much longer. I had to lie down or sit down or something. Had to get my head together. There was an old building across the street, and it looked like the front door was open. Maybe some juiceheads was in there. I didn't know, but I couldn't stay on the street much more. My arm was hurting too bad, and if that cop had really seen it was me, there would be more cops coming soon.

I felt like crying, like just running down the street and letting them shoot me—anything and everything at the same time. I was messed up bigtime and I knew it.

I saw two women walk over to the police car. Probably hookers out doing their stroll. The cop in the car was talking to them and then he got out and went around the back of the car. I looked to see if he had his gun in his hand. From where I was in the doorway I couldn't see too clear. He might have. I could feel my heart beating fast and

7

my right hand was shaking in my pocket. The cop and the two women walked a little way down the street, and he was up on his toes, trying to look into one of the building windows. I took a deep breath and moved from the doorway to behind a parked car. The street wasn't big and half the buildings didn't have nobody living in them, so it was dark except for the streetlight, and that wasn't working right. Nothing wasn't working right in my life.

I got across the street and into the doorway of the building I had been scoping. Looking down the street, I saw the cop and the two women were still together. The sound of another siren scared me. I couldn't tell where it was coming from. Keeping my eyes on the cop down the street, I pushed on the door behind me with my foot. It opened and I eased into the house.

The smell was terrible. Like somebody had been using it as a piss hole. It was dark except for the light from the cracked-open door. I saw some steps and started thinking about the roof. If I got to the roof, I could come down in another building, maybe even on another block. My left arm was pretty stiff and I didn't want to move it too much. I let go of the Nine I had been carrying since I left my house and fished around in my pockets for some matches. When I found some, I was scared to light them. Maybe the cop had seen me come into the building. Maybe he was just waiting outside for some backup before he came busting in the door.

I put the matches in the pocket with the Nine and started up the steps, walking close to the wall so they wouldn't creak too much.

The smell wasn't no better, but it changed a little as I got near the second floor. It was just that musty smell that old buildings have sometimes. I thought I smelled some vinegar too, so I thought there might have been some dopeheads shooting up in one of the rooms.

I stopped and lit a match, holding the book in my left hand and striking the match with my right. There was garbage on the floor and some piles of old plaster. I seen where the next steps was and started for them. I was being quiet because I didn't want to run into no dopehead or crazy homeless dude.

When I got to the third floor, I heard a sound. It

was people talking. I held my breath, trying to figure out if it was somebody who had come in after me or somebody already in the building. My heart was pumping big-time, a mile a minute, and I was feeling sick to my stomach as I leaned against the wall.

Maybe there was a way to figure out where the sound was coming from, but I didn't have that way in me. I was too scared to think good. I knew that if the sound was in the building, it wasn't no cops, so I started up the stairs again. Halfway up the next flight I saw a light coming from one of the doors. Then I heard the sound again and knew somebody had a television on.

If it was a homeless guy, it would be okay, unless he was crazy and had a knife or an axe or something. If I had to shoot him, the cops might hear it. If it was a doper it would be better. A doper might just be on a nod and might not even wake up.

When I got to the landing, I saw the open door and heard the sound from the television. Somebody talking about how to get some CDs for only $9.99. I slipped past the door and up the last flight to the roof door. I lit another match and saw crack vials and empty Baggies on the landing. I tried to turn the knob on the door leading to the roof, but it didn't move. I got long legs, so I put my back against the door and my foot against the post and pushed hard. Nothing. It didn't move.

For a moment I went crazy inside. I was in the building and couldn't get out to the roof. If anything went down, I knew I'd be trapped.

Calm down, man. Calm down. I tried to talk myself down. *Breathe slow. Breathe slow and get yourself together.* My mouth was dry, but I could feel the cold sweat dripping down my side from under my arm. My arm was hurt real bad. What was the use of keeping on running? If my arm got infected and I had to go to the hospital, they would have me. The bullet was still in my arm and they would just call the police. I imagined being handcuffed to a hospital bed and the cops bringing Rico in to identify me.

Yeah, that's him, I imagined Rico saying. *That's Lil J. He the one who shot the police officer.*

My eyes were closed and I opened them. Had to get out my head and get into the now. Had to think. Maybe there was a fire escape. If I could hit a fire escape, I could still make the roof.

I went down the stairs quick, but still near the bannister so I wouldn't make too much noise. If there was a doper in the apartment, he would know how to get out in a hurry. My hands were sweaty and I wiped them off on my pants leg. Had to look cool. Had to look confident.

I took a deep breath outside the door, then pushed it open quick.

It was a long room with a small television on a table in the corner. There was a dim light on the wall with one of those little yellow lampshades. About six feet in front of the television there was a chair and I could see the back of a dude's head. He could have been on a nod, or just sleeping. He wasn't moving.

I turned around to see what he was about.

"Stay where you are!"

I stopped, realized the Nine was still in my jacket pocket and took it out. I couldn't see any mirrors so I didn't know if he was seeing me or not. I knew I didn't want to have to shoot this sucker and get the cops pouring into the place, and with my left arm messed up I knew I just couldn't take him out if he had any heart.

"Who you, man?" I asked.

"Kelly," he said.

"Yo, I'm sorry I busted in on you," I said. "Some dudes said I did them wrong and they was chasing me. How I get to the roof?"

The guy didn't turn or nothing, just kept watching the television. I couldn't see his face, but his voice was young. He could have been just a little older than me, maybe eighteen or nineteen.

"There's a chair over there," he said. "Why don't you put your piece away and sit down."

"Man, I ain't got all day," I said, trying to get some bone in my voice. "The fire escape go to the roof?"

"You want to see yourself on television?"

I looked at the windows. There were shades over them and I figured maybe nobody could see the light from outside. I went over and looked out. There was a fire escape. I put my Nine back in my jacket and tried to lift the window.

"It's nailed shut," the guy said. "People don't be leaving their windows open in this neighborhood. You don't know that?"

"Yo, man, what you say your name was?"

"Kelly."

"Well, look, Kelly or Smelly or whatever your name is—I ain't nobody to be playing with," I said. "I'm the one with the Nine pointing at your head."

"Yeah, and you the one stuck in this building looking for a way out, ain't you?"

Kelly talked street, but I wasn't sure. Something about him wasn't from the 'hood. I wanted to go over to him and put the Nine against his neck, but for some reason I didn't think it was going to bother him. The sucker might have been crazy.

"You know a way out?" I asked.

"Why don't you cop a squat and check yourself out on the tube," Kelly said. He was looking at the television.

I looked at the television and saw the street below. It looked empty.

"You got the television hooked up to security cameras?" I asked.

"No."

"Then how come . . . ?" On the television there was a person moving across the street, wearing a dark jacket. He had one hand up by his side and the other in his jacket pocket. It was me.

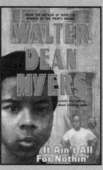